The Arcane Rebellion
Book Three

AURORA

Denis James

AURORA

The Arcane Rebellion Book Three

"Don't love someone who won't love you back."

Aurora Wildwood has spent months healing in the remote mountains of North Korea, learning to organize her trauma and control the magic that once nearly destroyed her. But when Tobias leads a desperate search team across international borders to find her, Aurora faces an impossible choice.

She could return to Bellwater Academy, to the people who love her and the community that needs her. She could rebuild the relationships her violence had shattered and reclaim her place as protector and leader. Or she could make the ultimate sacrifice—disappearing forever to protect Tobias from the one person who has hurt him most: herself.

As Aurora watches through scrying magic, she sees that Tobias has grown into the leader she always knew he could be. He's learned to love without controlling, to protect without possessing. He's built a real family with his team, based on trust instead of dependence.

Which means Aurora must decide: Is love about holding on, or is it about having the strength to let go?

Written by Denis James

COPYRIGHT 2025 BY DENIS JAMES

All rights reserved.

ARCANE REBELLION names, characters, and related indicia are trademarks of Writing by DJ, LLC copyright Denis James

All rights reserved.

No part of this publication may be reproduced, stored in a retrieval system, or transmitted in any form or by any means, electronic, mechanical, photocopying, recording, or otherwise, without written permission of the publisher. For information regarding permission, write to Writing by DJ, LLC: writingbydj@yahoo.com.

This book is a work of fiction. Names, characters, places, and incidents are either the product of the author's imagination or used fictitiously, and any resemblance to actual persons, living or dead, business establishments, events, or locales is entirely coincidental.

Book Cover Design and Interior Formatting by:
Aubrey Labitigan (facebook.com/designjai)

Dedications & Acknowledgements

In life, we get many chances to screw things up. To upset other people. To ruin perfectly good relationships, friendships, and familial ties. But we also get opportunities to forgive, to love, and to build new relationships and friendships.

My life has changed drastically in the last few years, for a variety of reasons. And I am so thankful to all of you who stuck by me, who supported me in this transition as I pursue my dream of being a writer.

I'm not always an easy person to love, but darn it, I'm trying to make it easier to do so.

Thank you all.

Much love,

Denis James

Contents

CHAPTER ZERO: The Arcane Rebellion: The Story So Far 2
CHAPTER ONE: Aurora's Descent 5
CHAPTER TWO: The Other Path 15
CHAPTER THREE: The Promise 25
CHAPTER FOUR: Reluctant Partners 33
CHAPTER FIVE: Unexpected Allies 39
CHAPTER SIX: Administrative Pressure 46
CHAPTER SEVEN: What Really Matters 54
CHAPTER EIGHT: The Weight of a Promise 60
CHAPTER NINE: Learning to Remember 66
CHAPTER TEN: One Memory at a Time 71
CHAPTER ELEVEN: The Investigation 76
CHAPTER TWELVE: Consequences 84
CHAPTER THIRTEEN: Questions Without Answers 93
CHAPTER FOURTEEN: The Mirror of Control 100
CHAPTER FIFTEEN: The Cost of Distance 107
CHAPTER SIXTEEN: Finding the Trail 116
CHAPTER SEVENTEEN: The Last Stand 125
CHAPTER EIGHTEEN: Borrowed Time 135
CHAPTER NINETEEN: Restoration 143
CHAPTER TWENTY: The Price of Clarity 149
CHAPTER TWENTY-ONE: The Trap 155
CHAPTER TWENTY-TWO: Poor Decisions 176
CHAPTER TWENTY-THREE: Aurora's Painful Choice 190
CHAPTER TWENTY-FOUR: The Final Truth 199
ABOUT THE AUTHOR 208

CHAPTER ZERO:
The Arcane Rebellion: The Story So Far

The story begins when Tobias Thornfield, a teacher at Jefferson High School, witnesses a devastating fire that consumes the entire school. The fire is no ordinary blaze—it's created by magical forces from the Arcane Rebellion, led by his best friend Hunter Diaz and his accomplices. Tobias reveals himself as a powerful mage specializing in water, wind, and lightning magic, and manages to save five students: Foxton Gray, Finnian Connor, twins Lyra and Elena Wilkins, and Darian Keen. When Darian dies from falling debris, Tobias makes the dangerous decision to resurrect him—a feat that nearly kills him in the process.

Tobias brings the survivors to Bellwater Cottage, where they meet Aurora Wildwood, the formidable leader of the Bellwater Mages who ascended to her position upon killing the previous leader, per the bylaws. Aurora is a master of earth magic with a particular talent for plant manipulation, but she struggles with severe anger management issues. Despite her good intentions, she has a pattern of losing control—strangling Elena with a sunflower when the girl makes a disrespectful comment about plant magic, and later massacring an entire police force with an earthquake when they threaten her group. Indeed, Aurora struggles with severe anger management issues that lead to increasingly violent outbursts when challenged or stressed.

The Bellwater Mages operate as teachers at Bellwater Academy, secretly training magic users while maintaining their cover. Aurora serves as the school's guidance counselor under the tyrannical Principal Percival Ion. The group includes Sabrina Braithwaite (science teacher and fire magic specialist), Lucien Rodson (art/music teacher and wind magic specialist), Agatha O'Connor (elderly English teacher and water magic specialist), and Matilda Carrington (special education teacher who trains new apprentices).

When Tobias substitutes for the injured Agatha, Principal Ion fires him for expressing anti-establishment views to students. This leads to a mission where Tobias and newcomer Odion Montgomery—a math teacher learning water magic—infiltrate an Arcane Rebellion base. They discover the Rebellion has detailed files on all Bellwater members, suggesting a mole within their ranks.

Hunter, revealed to be working with Principal Ion, lures Tobias into a trap. Ion shoots Tobias, but Hunter kills Ion in a fit of rage and remorse. During Tobias's hospitalization, Aurora's group fractured over her violent actions. Despite Tobias and elderly Agatha supporting her, Sabrina Braithwaite successfully orchestrates Aurora's removal as leader, taking control of the Bellwater Mages herself.

Meanwhile, Sabrina and Lucien are revealed as the true moles—they've been secretly leading the Arcane Rebellion all along while posing as loyal Bellwater members. Their orchestration of Aurora's downfall was part of a larger plan to seize control of both organizations.

When Hunter once again confronts Tobias. Tobias had to make a choice: save himself and let his student Foxton be killed by Hunter or allow himself to be defeated and captured by his former best friend. He chose to save Foxton, resulting in Hunter kidnapping and imprisoning him.

Importantly, Hunter never killed Tobias despite his orders from Sabrina and Lucien being crystal clear. Instead, he kidnapped and imprisoned him in a remote cottage, using magic-draining chains to keep him powerless and feeling completely alone and isolated from those who love him while lying to the Rebellion about completing his mission. Hunter's motivations are complex—partly romantic obsession, partly a misguided attempt to protect Tobias from Aurora's growing instability, and partly his own internal conflict about his loyalties.

Meanwhile, Tobias's former students—Lyra, Elena, and Darian—are tasked to train with Hunter to become weapons against their former teachers. The teenagers, traumatized and angry about losing their families, initially embrace this training but eventually turn against both sides when they realize they're being manipulated. Elena especially seems distraught about having to work with the man who killed their friends and families just to survive.

Several weeks later, Tobias finally breaks through to Hunter. The pair of them discover that Aurora, now Principal of Bellwater Academy following Ion's death, has been systematically torturing Marina—a blue-haired water magic specialist from the Arcane Rebellion—to extract information about Tobias's whereabouts. Aurora and Odion had kidnapped Marina during their desperate search, with Aurora's mental state deteriorating as she became increasingly violent and unstable. Her desperation to find Tobias leads her to increasingly extreme measures, including torturing an innocent person and making decisions that alienate even her closest allies. When confronted with her actions, she shows little remorse and refuses to acknowledge wrongdoing, ultimately driving away both Odion and virtually all of her former supporters.

In a tragic turn, Darian—the boy Tobias once resurrected—chooses death again, and Tobias grants his wish by killing him with lightning magic.

The story ends with Tobias and Odion rescuing Aurora from the Rebellion's stronghold, but the damage to relationships appears irreparable. Aurora has lost the trust and respect of almost everyone around her, including Tobias, who finally sees her for who she truly is. As the book concludes, Aurora has teleported away, alone and abandoned by those she once led.

CHAPTER ONE:
Aurora's Descent

Aurora Wildwood woke to the sight of withered pine needles falling like snow around her makeshift camp. What was green and alive when she collapsed here three days ago now stood as skeletal monuments to her presence. The trees surrounding her clearing drooped with blackened branches, their bark cracked and oozing dark sap. Even the hardy mountain grasses shriveled into brittle stalks that crunched under the slightest movement.

She pushed herself up from the frozen ground, her body protesting. The torn remnants of what was once an elegant red sweater hung loose on her frame. She lost so much weight that her clothes seemed to belong to someone else entirely. Her hands, once manicured and pristine, were now stained black with sap and soil, the nails broken and caked with dirt from her unconscious attempts to burrow into the earth while she slept.

The silence was absolute. Even the wind seemed afraid to disturb this place.

Aurora staggered to her feet, her legs trembling from malnutrition and exhaustion. The dead zone extended at least thirty feet in every direction, and she saw where her magic carved small fissures in the earth—jagged scars that spoke to the chaos churning inside her.

Even the earth itself rejects me now, she thought bitterly, running a shaking hand through her matted hair. When had she last bathed? Last eaten something that hadn't withered at her touch? The days blurred together in this remote corner of North Korea, far from any civilization that might suffer from her presence.

She chose this isolation deliberately. After teleporting away from Bellwater, after seeing the horror in Odion's eyes, the disappointment in Tobias's face, and hearing the anger in Hunter's voice, she knew she needed to disappear. The massacre. The police officers laying broken in the street. Elena's terrified face as the sunflower wrapped around her throat.

A sob escaped her lips, and the ground beneath her feet cracked in response. A hairline fracture split the frozen earth, spreading outward like a spider's web. Aurora stumbled backward, but there was nowhere to go that her influence wouldn't follow.

She needed water. Food. But every stream she approached turned stagnant within moments of her arrival. Every plant she tried to forage crumbled to ash in her hands. Her earth magic, once a source of pride and nurturing growth, became a curse that drained life from everything around her. The irony wasn't lost on her, she who always prided herself on making things grow was now a walking blight.

Aurora forced herself to move deeper into the forest, each step leaving small dead patches in the moss. Her stomach cramped with hunger, a constant companion these past weeks. She managed to sustain herself partially through the magical energy she was unconsciously draining from the plant life, but it wasn't enough. Her body was consuming itself, and soon even that wouldn't be sufficient to keep her alive.

Good, she thought with savage satisfaction. *Maybe that's how this should end.*

The trees here were older, their trunks thick and gnarled with age.

AURORA

For a moment, Aurora allowed herself to hope they might resist her influence longer than the younger growth. She approached a massive pine, its bark scarred by decades of wind and weather. Perhaps she could lean against it for a moment, rest without—

The tree shuddered the moment she made contact. Aurora snatched her hand away, but it was too late. She watched in horror as the ancient pine began to wither from the point of contact outward, its needles browning and falling like tears. Within minutes, a tree that stood for perhaps a century was reduced to a brittle husk.

"No," she whispered, backing away. "No, no, *no!*"

The word became a scream that tore from her throat, raw and desperate. The earth responded to her anguish with a violent tremor that sent rocks tumbling down the mountainside. Birds roosting in distant trees took flight in panicked clouds, their cries echoing across the valley below.

Aurora fell to her knees among the falling debris, her hands pressed to her temples. The memories came flooding back with crystal clarity. Tobias's disappointed face when she attacked Elena. Odion's quiet disapproval. The way Sabrina smiled as she took Aurora's leadership away, as though she'd been waiting for the opportunity all along.

And Marina. Sweet, terrified Marina with her blue hair and water magic, chained in that basement while Aurora demanded answers she didn't have. The way the young woman whimpered when Aurora's thorns bit into her skin. The blood on her hands—not metaphorical, but real, sticky, and warm.

"I destroy everything I touch," Aurora said aloud, her voice hoarse from disuse and dehydration. The admission hung in the air like a condemnation. "Everything. Everyone."

She thought of Tobias, probably still recovering from the gunshot wound she indirectly caused. Of the students who trusted her before her violence drove them away. Of the police officers who would never go home to their families because she lost control for a handful of seconds.

The tremors intensified as her shame deepened, cracks spreading through the mountainside. Somewhere in the distance, she heard the groaning protest of shifting stone, the rumble of a small landslide. She was poisoning the very ground beneath her feet, and she couldn't stop.

Aurora crawled through the devastation she created, desperate for any source of water that might have escaped her influence. Her throat felt like sandpaper, her lips cracked and bleeding. She hadn't realized how far her magic spread until she crested a small ridge and saw it: a stream, clear and bright, cutting through a grove of healthy evergreens.

Hope flared in her chest. The water sang as it flowed over smooth stones, untouched by her presence. Aurora half-ran, half-fell down the slope toward it, her legs giving out completely as she reached the bank. She collapsed onto her hands and knees at the water's edge, so close she could feel the cool mist on her face.

The moment her skin touched the surface, the change was instantaneous.

The crystal-clear water turned murky brown, then black. Fish floated to the surface belly-up, their silver scales dulling to gray. The healthy trees along the bank began to droop, their needles falling into the poisoned stream. Within seconds, what had been a source of life became another monument to her destructive presence.

Aurora's scream of frustration and despair echoed off the mountains, carrying with it every ounce of magical energy she had left. The earth split beneath her hands, a chasm opening in the streambed that swallowed the corrupted water in great, gurgling gasps. Trees toppled as their roots were severed, crashing into the growing fissure with sounds like thunder.

She knelt in the ruins of what had been her last hope, sobbing into her blackened hands. The tremors continued for long minutes, strong enough to be felt for miles in every direction. Somewhere, animals were fleeing. Somewhere, the mountain itself was reshaping in response to her breakdown.

Aurora didn't care. Let it all fall. Let the whole world crack and crumble. It would be no more than she deserved.

"I destroy everything I touch," she whispered to the devastation around her. "Even mercy would be wasted on me."

The darkness crept in at the edges of her vision as exhaustion and dehydration finally claimed her. Her last conscious thought was a bitter laugh at the irony—she who had always been so strong, so in control, was going to die alone in a foreign forest, killed by her own magic.

The tremors gradually subsided as unconsciousness took her, leaving only the sound of settling debris and the distant cry of displaced wildlife. In the growing silence, Aurora Wildwood lay motionless among the ruins of her own making, her breathing shallow and her skin pale as winter frost.

* * *

The old woman had felt the tremors from thirty miles away.

She'd been tending her own small garden—a careful collection of hardy mountain plants that could survive in this remote corner of North Korea—when the first shockwave had rattled her modest shelter. At first, she assumed it was a natural earthquake, but the pattern was wrong. Too emotional. Too focused. The earth itself was screaming.

The woman packed her supplies without hesitation, following the magical signature like a bloodhound following a scent. She walked through similar devastation before, decades ago, when her own magic had spiraled beyond control and left a trail of broken minds in its wake. She recognized this particular flavor of magical crisis—the way the very ground seemed to recoil from whatever had caused this destruction.

What she found was worse than she expected.

The woman lying unconscious in the ruined streambed was clearly dying. Severe dehydration, malnutrition, and magical exhaustion had left her looking like a skeleton wrapped in torn cloth. But it was the circle of death surrounding her that truly revealed the scope of the crisis. This wasn't just magical exhaustion. This was complete loss of control, magic feeding on everything around it to keep its user barely alive.

The woman approached cautiously, her feet silent on the broken ground. She was old enough to remember when such displays of uncontrolled power had been more common, before the magical communities had learned better ways to handle trauma. This young woman trapped in a feedback loop of self-destruction.

"What happened to you, child?" Raven murmured, kneeling beside the unconscious figure. Up close, she could see the telltale signs of someone who had been living rough for weeks. The hands were those of someone who had once taken pride in her appearance, now reduced to desperate survival.

Aurora's eyes fluttered open at the sound of a voice. For a moment, she stared uncomprehendingly at the weathered face above her, convinced she was hallucinating from starvation. The woman was clearly Native American, with silver-streaked black hair braided down her back and eyes that seemed to hold decades of patient wisdom. She wore practical clothing suitable for mountain survival, but there was something in her manner that spoke of careful control.

"You're not real," Aurora croaked, her voice barely a whisper.

"Real enough," the woman replied gently. "And you're lucky I found you when I did. Another few hours and this would have been a recovery mission instead of a rescue."

AURORA

Aurora tried to push herself up, but her arms gave out immediately. "You need to leave," she managed. "Everything I touch dies. You should go before—"

"Before what? Before your magic kills me? Me, Raven, controller of memories?" The woman's tone was matter of fact rather than fearful. "Child, your earth magic can't hurt me any more than I let it."

The words penetrated Aurora's fevered consciousness slowly. Another mage. Someone who understood what she was going through, who might not run screaming from the destruction she caused.

"How did you—" Aurora began, but the world tilted sideways as unconsciousness claimed her again.

Raven worked quickly, pulling a carefully prepared vial from her pack. The liquid inside was clear as water but tasted of mountain herbs and something harder to define—the essence of peaceful sleep. She managed to get several drops between Aurora's cracked lips before settling back to wait.

The effect was almost immediate. The constant tremors in the earth around Aurora stilled as her magic finally calmed. The desperate feeding pattern that had been draining life from everything nearby ceased, allowing what remained of the local plant life to begin its slow recovery.

When Aurora woke again, it was in a place she didn't recognize. The air was warm and dry, carrying the scent of burning wood and herbal tea. She was lying on a simple cot, covered with clean blankets that felt impossibly soft against her skin. For the first time in weeks, her body wasn't wrecked with constant tremors.

"Good, you're awake." The same voice from before, calm and steady. Raven was sitting across the small space, stirring something that smelled like soup. The shelter was basic but well-maintained—stone walls built into the mountainside, a small fireplace providing warmth and light, supplies arranged with military precision.

Aurora tried to sit up and was surprised when her body actually obeyed. The crushing exhaustion was still there, but the desperate, gnawing hunger had eased. "What did you do to me?"

"Bought you some time," Raven replied simply. "Your magic was consuming everything around you because your mind couldn't process what you'd been through. I've created some temporary barriers in your memory—not erasing anything, just organizing it so the trauma doesn't trigger constant magical surges."

"You can do that?" Aurora's voice was still hoarse, but stronger than before.

"Memory magic is useful for more than just reading minds," Raven said, bringing over a bowl of thin broth. "I can help people compartmentalize trauma, create mental walls that allow for healing without forgetting. But it's temporary. Eventually, you'll need to face what happened properly."

Aurora accepted the bowl with shaking hands, the warm liquid feeling like salvation against her parched throat. "Why?" she asked between careful sips. "Why help me? You don't know what I've done."

Raven settled back in her chair, studying Aurora with those knowing eyes. "I know enough. The destruction pattern outside tells me you've lost people you cared about. The magical signature suggests you've done things you regret deeply. The fact that you isolated yourself here tells me you think you deserve to die for it."

"I do deserve to die for it," Aurora said flatly. "I killed innocent people. I tortured a young woman for information she didn't have. I attacked a teenage girl with magic because she questioned me. I'm not a victim—I'm the monster."

Raven was quiet for a long moment, then said, "Monsters don't feel shame."

"What?"

AURORA

"Monsters don't isolate themselves in remote forests to die rather than risk hurting others. Monsters don't destroy themselves with guilt over their actions. You made terrible choices, yes. But the fact that you recognize them as terrible, that you're willing to pay with your life rather than risk repeating them…that's not what monsters do."

Aurora stared into her soup, tears falling silently into the broth. "You don't understand. I lost control. I killed police officers because I was angry. I nearly strangled a student with a sunflower because she questioned my methods. I tortured that poor girl with thorns and vines until she was bleeding from dozens of wounds. I became everything I swore I'd never be."

"I lost control once too," Raven said quietly. "Nearly destroyed everything I loved. Spent twenty years hiding afterward, convinced I was too dangerous to be around other people. It took me a long time to learn that healing doesn't mean forgetting. It means learning to carry the weight without being crushed by it."

Aurora looked up sharply. "What did you do?"

"That's a story for another day. Right now, we need to focus on you." Raven leaned forward, her expression serious but not unkind. "I can teach you techniques for managing trauma-induced magical instability. Your magic isn't broken, but your mind is carrying too much weight. I won't force this on you. You can choose to die here if that's what you want. Or you can choose to live and make amends."

The choice hung in the air between them like a challenge. Aurora had spent weeks convinced that death was the only way to ensure she never hurt anyone again. But hearing it spoken aloud, presented as a real option rather than an inevitable conclusion, made her hesitate.

"I don't know if I can be saved," she whispered.

"Neither do I," Raven admitted. "But I'm willing to try if you are. The question is whether you want to give yourself the chance to find out."

Aurora closed her eyes, feeling the artificial calm Raven's memory magic had provided. For the first time in weeks, her thoughts weren't a chaotic spiral of guilt and self-recrimination. In this strange, temporary peace, she could almost imagine a future where she wasn't defined solely by her worst moments.

"If I agree," she said slowly, "I'm not promising forgiveness. I'm not promising redemption. I may be beyond saving."

"I understand," Raven replied. "But if you're going to make that decision, it should be based on a clear understanding of who you are and what you've done, not on the distorted perspective of trauma and magical exhaustion."

Aurora was quiet for a long time, staring into the fire. Finally, she nodded. "All right. But if I hurt you—if I lose control again—"

"Then we'll deal with that when it happens," Raven said firmly. "For now, let's focus on getting you strong enough to think clearly. Everything else can wait."

CHAPTER TWO:
The Other Path

Aurora awoke to the scent of mountain herbs and something else—hope, perhaps, though she barely recognized it anymore. For the first time in weeks, she had slept without nightmares. No visions of police officers falling under her earthquake. No memories of Elena's terrified face as the sunflower tightened around her throat. Just peaceful, dreamless darkness.

She sat up carefully, testing her body's response. The crushing exhaustion was still there, but the desperate tremors that had wracked her frame for weeks were gone. Her magic felt different too. Not absent but changed somehow. Like a wild animal that had finally stopped thrashing against its cage.

"Good morning," Raven said from across the small shelter. She was preparing something that smelled like herbal tea, her movements precise and calming. "How do you feel?"

"Different," Aurora admitted, accepting the warm cup Raven offered. The liquid tasted of pine needles and something sweeter. Perhaps honey, though she couldn't imagine where Raven would have found it in this remote place. "My magic... it's not fighting me anymore."

"The memory barriers are holding," Raven explained, settling into her chair. "Your traumatic memories are still there, but they're organized now. Filed away where they can't trigger constant magical surges."

Aurora stared at the older woman, curiosity finally overriding her exhaustion. "I don't understand how you can do this. I thought magic came from feeling loved, from connection. How can you manipulate memories?"

Raven studied Aurora's face. Then she said, "Tell me what you know about magic."

"Magic flows from emotion—from feeling valued, loved, connected to others. The stronger those feelings, the stronger the magic. When someone feels isolated or unloved, their magic fades." Aurora recited the lessons she learned at Bellwater, the fundamental truths that had shaped her understanding for years. "Most magic focuses on the elements—earth, fire, water, wind, lightning. Combat magic."

"And where did you learn this?"

"From my predecessor at Bellwater. And before that, from the teachers who trained him. It's common knowledge among magical practitioners."

Raven nodded slowly. "Common knowledge within your organizations, perhaps. But tell me, Aurora—how many magical organizations exist in the world?"

The question caught Aurora off guard. "Two, of course. Bellwater and the Arcane Rebellion."

"Are you certain?"

Aurora opened her mouth to respond, then closed it again. How could she be certain? She never looked beyond those two groups, never questioned whether there might be others. The Bellwater Mages and the Arcane Rebellion had seemed to encompass the entire magical world.

AURORA

"I see you're beginning to understand," Raven said gently. "Your organizations only taught what they knew. Magic born from love and connection, focused on destruction and combat. But there are other paths, Aurora. Paths your teachers never discovered."

"What kind of paths?"

Instead of answering directly, Raven stood and moved to a small mirror mounted on the stone wall. "Let me show you something," she said, placing her palm flat against the glass. "I'm going to demonstrate on myself, so you can see how memory magic works."

Aurora watched, fascinated, as Raven's reflection began to shift and change. The glass showed not Raven as she was now, but Raven as she had been decades ago. Younger, with long black hair unmarked by silver, wearing clothes Aurora didn't recognize.

"This is from twenty-one years ago," Raven said, her voice taking on a distant quality. "I was living in Arizona then, trying to raise my son alone after his father left us. I was... not handling it well."

The image in the mirror moved, showing the younger Raven in what looked like a modest kitchen. A small, oddly familiar-looking boy sat at a wooden table, perhaps six or seven years old, with dark hair and features that clearly marked him as Raven's child. He was crying about something—Aurora couldn't hear the words, but she could see the distress in his small face.

"I was exhausted, overwhelmed," Raven continued, her voice carefully controlled. "Working three jobs to keep food on the table, getting maybe four hours of sleep a night. My earth magic was all I had that felt like power in my life, and I was using it for everything. Growing vegetables when I couldn't afford groceries, making flowers bloom to cheer him up, anything to feel like I had some control."

Aurora watched the scene unfold with growing dread. She could see where this was going.

The young Raven in the mirror grew agitated, her gestures becoming more animated as she spoke to the crying child. Whatever he'd done—spilled something, perhaps, or broken something—it was clearly the last straw in what had been a very long day.

"I lost my temper," Raven said quietly. "Completely lost control."

Aurora gasped as thorny vines erupted from the kitchen floor, wrapping around the little boy's arms and legs. Just like Elena. Just like what she'd done to that terrified girl who only made a sarcastic comment. The child's tears turned to screams of terror as the thorns bit into his skin, and the younger Raven seemed to watch in horror as her magic spiraled beyond her control.

"I couldn't stop it," Raven whispered. "The vines kept growing, getting tighter. My son was bleeding, and I couldn't make it stop. My earth magic was feeding on my rage, my frustration, my exhaustion."

Aurora's hands flew to her mouth as she watched the scene play out. This was exactly what she'd done to Elena, what she'd been terrified of doing again. The parallel was so perfect it made her stomach turn.

But then something changed. In the mirror, the younger Raven suddenly went completely still. Her eyes widened with something beyond horror—a desperate, primal need to save her child. And at that moment, something unprecedented happened.

The thorny vines stopped growing. Not because Raven had regained control of her earth magic, Aurora could see that the chaotic energy was still swirling around the room. But something else had taken over. Something new.

"That was the moment," Raven said softly. "The exact moment I discovered I could do something no one had ever taught me. I reached into my son's mind and... organized what he was experiencing."

Aurora watched in amazement as the terrified expression faded from the little boy's face. The vines were still there, still wrapped around him, but suddenly he looked calm. Peaceful, even. As though the traumatic experience was happening to someone else.

"I didn't erase his memory of the attack," Raven clarified. "I couldn't do that yet—that came later. But I could compartmentalize it, file it away where it wouldn't dominate his immediate experience. Create distance between him and the trauma."

The vines withered away as Raven's earth magic finally calmed, and the little boy looked around in confusion. Aurora could see that he remembered being hurt, but it no longer seemed to cause him active distress.

"How is that possible?" Aurora breathed.

Raven touched the mirror again, and the image faded back to her current reflection. "Because trauma doesn't just break us, Aurora. When we survive what should have destroyed us, it opens pathways in our minds that weren't there before. Your organizations teach magic born from love and connection—but there's another path. Magic born from surviving the un-survivable."

Aurora felt something shift in her understanding, like a door opening in her mind. "Trauma-born magic."

"Exactly." Raven returned to her chair, her expression serious but not unkind. "The magic you learned at Bellwater served you well when you felt secure and loved. Earth magic for nurturing growth, creating beautiful gardens, defending the people you care about. But that magic failed you when everything fell apart, didn't it?"

Aurora nodded, thinking of the weeks in this forest when her earth magic had become a curse, draining life instead of nurturing it.

"That's because you needed different tools," Raven continued. "Magic that could help you survive impossible circumstances. Magic that could help you rebuild from nothing."

"The life-draining," Aurora said slowly. "When I couldn't control my earth magic anymore, when it started feeding on everything around me..."

"That wasn't a loss of control. That was evolution. Your magic was trying to keep you alive when you had no other resources. It was adapting to circumstances your peaceful earth magic wasn't designed to handle."

Aurora stared at Raven, her mind reeling. "You're saying my trauma is... making me stronger?"

"I'm saying trauma can forge tools you never knew you needed," Raven corrected gently. "Whether that makes you stronger depends on what you choose to do with those tools."

"What happened to your son?" Aurora asked quietly.

Raven's expression darkened. "I knew I was too dangerous to stay with him. My earth magic was still unstable, and I discovered I could manipulate memories—do you have any idea how terrifying that is? I could accidentally rewrite someone's entire personality without meaning to."

Aurora thought about the power Raven had just demonstrated, the way she'd been able to organize Aurora's own traumatic memories. The potential for abuse was staggering.

"So, I made a choice," Raven continued. "I used my new abilities to erase his memories of the attack, then I left. I convinced myself it was mercy, that he was better off not remembering what I'd done to him."

"Did you ever see him again?"

"No." The word was heavy with decades of regret. "Leaving him was the most loving thing I could do, but it was also the greatest mistake of my life. I chose to protect him from me instead of learning to control myself for him."

Aurora absorbed this in silence. Here was someone who truly understood the weight of having hurt someone innocent, someone who made the ultimate sacrifice to prevent further harm. And yet...

AURORA

"How do you still have magic?" Aurora asked. "If you've been isolated for twenty-one years, how do you still feel loved enough to maintain your abilities?"

Raven smiled sadly. "Because leaving him was an act of love. The most painful, selfless thing I've ever done. My magic doesn't come from receiving love anymore, Aurora. It comes from loving him enough to stay away."

The implications hit Aurora like a physical blow. Magic sustained by sacrifice rather than connection. Power that grew stronger through loss rather than gain. It challenged everything she thought she knew about how magical abilities worked.

"This is just the beginning," Raven said, seeming to read Aurora's thoughts. "Memory magic, life magic, healing magic. There are entire disciplines your organizations never discovered because they were afraid to explore what trauma could teach them."

Aurora felt overwhelmed by the possibilities, but also terrified. "What if I hurt people with these new abilities? What if I become even more dangerous?"

"That's always a risk," Raven admitted. "Trauma-born magic is powerful precisely because it's forged in extremity. But the question isn't whether you might hurt people, you've already done that. The question is what you're going to do now."

Aurora was quiet for a long time, staring into her tea. Finally, she asked, "Could you teach me? These memory techniques, this trauma-born magic?"

"I can teach you the basics," Raven replied. "But only if you truly want to learn. This isn't about deserving new abilities, Aurora. This is about what you need to survive and eventually make amends."

"I don't know if I can be trusted with more power."

"Trust isn't something you have or don't have," Raven said firmly.

"It's something you build through consistent choices. Every time you choose healing over destruction, growth over stagnation, you become a little more trustworthy."

Aurora closed her eyes, feeling the artificial calm Raven's memory barriers provided. For the first time since leaving Bellwater, she could think clearly about her options. Death was still possible; Raven wouldn't stop her if that's what she chose. But there was another path now, one she never imagined.

"What would you teach me first?"

"The same thing I just demonstrated," Raven said. "How to organize your own traumatic memories so they inform your choices without controlling them. How to file the pain where it can't trigger magical surges, while still learning from your mistakes."

"Will it hurt?"

"Yes," Raven said honestly. "Facing trauma always hurts. But right now, those memories are controlling you. If you learn to control them instead, you'll have the mental clarity to decide what kind of person you want to become."

Aurora thought about the weeks she spent in this forest, consumed by guilt and self-hatred, her magic spiraling into uncontrolled destruction. Then she thought about the moment when Raven had organized her memories, the blessed quiet that had followed.

"I want to try," she said finally. "But if I hurt you—"

"Then we'll deal with that when it happens," Raven interrupted. "For now, let's focus on getting you strong enough to think clearly about your choices."

Raven moved to a small wooden box Aurora hadn't noticed before. Inside were what looked like smooth river stones, each one carved with symbols Aurora didn't recognize.

AURORA

"These will help you practice," Raven explained, selecting three stones. "Each one represents a different type of memory—trauma, guilt, and regret. We're going to start by teaching you to separate them from each other."

"How?"

"Close your eyes and think about Elena—the girl you attacked with the sunflower."

Aurora's body tensed immediately, her magic beginning to respond to the surge of guilt and shame.

"Now," Raven said calmly, "instead of trying to push the memory away, I want you to examine it. What exactly happened? What did you do, and why did you do it?"

Aurora forced herself to relive that moment. Elena questioning her methods, the surge of fury that had followed, the sunflower springing to life around the girl's throat. But this time, instead of drowning in the emotion, she tried to observe it clinically.

"Good," Raven murmured. "Now take that memory and imagine placing it in a file cabinet. Label the file clearly: 'Elena, sunflower attack, my loss of control.' Put it where you can find it when you need to learn from it, but where it won't constantly intrude on your thoughts."

Aurora struggled with the concept at first. Her trauma felt too big, too overwhelming to simply file. But gradually, she began to understand what Raven meant. The memory didn't disappear; it just became manageable.

"How do you feel?" Raven asked after several minutes.

Aurora opened her eyes in surprise. The memory of Elena was still there, but it no longer felt like a wound being constantly torn open. She could think about what she'd done without being consumed by it.

"Different," she said. "Clearer."

"That's just the beginning," Raven said. "True healing will take time, and you'll need to practice these techniques until they become second nature. But you've taken the first step."

Aurora looked out the small window of the shelter, where she could see the forest beginning its slow recovery from her magical rampage. Trees that had been withering were showing tiny signs of new growth. The stream she'd poisoned was running clear again.

"Do you think I can become someone worthy of these new abilities?" she asked quietly.

Raven studied her for a long time. "I think you can become someone who chooses what to do with them wisely," she responded. "Whether that makes you worthy isn't for me to decide."

Aurora nodded, understanding the distinction. Worthiness would have to be earned through her actions, not granted through her suffering.

CHAPTER THREE:
The Promise

"Good morning," Raven said from her usual spot by the small fire. She was preparing what smelled like actual breakfast—eggs and some kind of mountain herb that made Aurora's mouth water. "How do you feel today?"

"Stronger," Aurora admitted, accepting the plate Raven offered. The eggs were warm and perfectly seasoned, a luxury she forgot existed. "My magic feels... quieter. Less like it's trying to consume everything around me."

"The memory barriers are holding well," Raven observed, settling into her chair with her own breakfast. "Your traumatic memories are properly contained now. They're still there when you need to learn from them, but they're not controlling your magical responses."

Aurora ate in contemplative silence, marveling at how clear her thoughts felt. For the first time since leaving Bellwater, she could think about Tobias without being overwhelmed by crushing guilt. She could remember the police massacre without her magic immediately responding with tremors and destruction.

"I think I'm ready," she said finally.

Raven raised an eyebrow. "Ready for what?"

"To try the memory organization techniques myself. To learn how to do what you've been doing for me." Aurora set down her empty plate, feeling more determined than she had in weeks. "I can't rely on your memory barriers forever. I need to learn how to manage my own trauma."

Raven studied her for a long moment, then nodded slowly. "We can try. But we'll start small; something foundational but not actively traumatic. Something that brings you comfort rather than pain."

"What did you have in mind?"

"Let's work with your feelings about Tobias," Raven suggested, moving to retrieve her collection of memory stones. "Not the recent events, those are still too volatile. But something earlier, something that represents your care for him without the complications of recent failures."

Aurora felt a warm flutter of affection at the mention of Tobias's name. Yes, that was perfect. Despite everything that had happened, her love for him remained uncomplicated at its core. "I can do that."

"Good." Raven arranged three stones on the small table between them. "Close your eyes and think about your earliest memory of caring for him, of wanting to protect him. Something that shows why he matters to you so much."

Aurora closed her eyes obediently, expecting to find herself thinking about their early days at Bellwater Academy. Perhaps the first time she'd seen him struggling with depression, or the moment she realized how much he needed someone to watch over him. Those were good memories, foundational but not traumatic.

"Now," Raven said softly, "I'm going to help you visualize the filing process. Feel my magic guiding yours, helping you organize what you're experiencing."

Aurora felt Raven's presence in her mind, gentle but sure. It was a strange sensation, like having someone help you organize a cluttered room.

AURORA

She relaxed in the guidance, trusting Raven to help her learn this new skill.

But instead of the academy memories she expected, Aurora felt Raven's magic pulling her somewhere else entirely. Deeper. Much deeper.

"This isn't what I expected to find," Raven murmured, her voice sounding distant now.

Aurora tried to redirect her thoughts toward more recent memories, but Raven's magic had latched onto something fundamental. Something buried so deep it felt like bedrock in her mind.

And suddenly, Aurora wasn't in the mountain shelter anymore.

She was six years old again, standing in a warm, sunlit kitchen that smelled of baking bread and her mother's lavender soap. Her parents were talking quietly with another couple. A man with kind eyes and a woman with Tobias's exact smile. And there, toddling around the kitchen in a diaper and nothing else, was the most beautiful little boy Aurora had ever seen.

"Rora!" two-year-old Tobias squealed, reaching chubby arms up toward her. He couldn't quite pronounce her name yet, but the way he said it made her feel special, important.

"Hi, Toby," young Aurora said, scooping him up and spinning him around until he giggled. He was so small, so perfect, with dark hair that stuck up in every direction and brown eyes that trusted her completely.

But the adults were talking in hushed, worried tones, and even at six, Aurora could sense that something was wrong. Very wrong.

"The curse is spreading faster than we thought," Tobias's father was saying to Aurora's parents. "We have maybe days, not weeks."

"There has to be something we can do," Aurora's mother replied, her voice tight with concern. "Some way to break it, or transfer it, or—"

"No." Tobias's mother shook her head, tears streaming down her face. "We've tried everything. We're not going to survive this."

Adult Aurora, watching from within her childhood memory, felt her stomach drop. She'd never known how her parents' friends had died. Tobias had always just said they died when he was very young, and she never pressed for details.

"What about Tobias?" her father asked quietly.

"He's too young to be affected by the curse," Tobias's father said. "But he'll need guidance when his magic manifests. He'll need someone who understands our world."

"We'll take him," Aurora's mother said immediately. "Of course we'll take him."

But Tobias's mother was shaking her head again. "You have your own children to think about. And with the Rebellion hunting down magical families... it's not safe to take in orphans. They'll know he's not yours."

Young Aurora didn't understand most of what the adults were saying, but she understood that Toby's parents were going away and wouldn't be coming back. The thought made her chest hurt in a way she never felt before.

"Aurora, sweetheart," Tobias's mother called softly. "Can you come here for a moment?"

Aurora set Toby down gently and walked over to the grown-ups, her small hands twisted nervously in her dress. Tobias's mother knelt down, so they were eye-level, her face kind but desperately sad.

"Aurora, I need you to do something very important for me," she said, her voice shaking slightly. "Can you do that?"

Aurora nodded solemnly. She wanted to help, wanted to do something to make the sad lady feel better.

"I need you to promise me something about Toby," Tobias's mother continued. "He's going to go live with other people when we... when we can't take care of him anymore. But someday, when you're both older, you're going to find each other again. Magic has a way of bringing the right people together."

AURORA

Aurora glanced back at little Tobias, who was now sitting on the floor playing with wooden spoons he pulled from a drawer. He looked so small, so innocent. The thought of him being sad or scared made Aurora's chest hurt even worse.

"When that happens," Tobias's mother said, gripping Aurora's small hands in her own, "I need you to promise me you'll always take care of him. No matter what happens, no matter how hard it gets, you'll keep our Toby safe. Can you promise me that?"

Six-year-old Aurora looked into the dying woman's desperate eyes and felt the weight of something enormous settling on her shoulders. She didn't understand what she was promising, not really. She just knew that this was important, that Toby needed someone to protect him.

"I promise," she said solemnly. "I'll keep Toby safe forever and ever."

Tobias's mother pulled her into a fierce hug, sobbing into her hair. "Thank you, sweetheart. Thank you so much."

Adult Aurora, still trapped in the memory, felt like she couldn't breathe. This was it. This was the moment that had defined her entire life. She'd been six years old, making a promise she couldn't possibly understand to people who were about to die. She'd always known, somewhere deep down, that there was a reason for her fierce protectiveness of Tobias. But her mind had buried the specifics, filing away the trauma of that day while keeping the promise intact. Now, seeing it clearly for the first time in decades, she understood why she'd never been able to explain her devotion to him. It hadn't been a choice—it had been a sacred vow made by a child who then spent thirty years forgetting why she made it. She'd never known herself as separate from this responsibility. Every protective instinct, every controlling decision, every moment of fierce devotion to Tobias—it all traced back to this moment. To a little girl who promised to keep someone safe 'forever and ever.'

"Aurora." Raven's voice seemed to come from very far away. "We need to organize this memory. File it away where it can inform your choices without controlling them."

"No." The word came out as a gasp, then stronger. "No, you can't—"

"Aurora, this is exactly the kind of foundational memory that needs to be properly contained. It's controlling every decision you make—"

"This isn't just a memory!" Aurora's eyes snapped open, and she found herself back in the mountain shelter, trembling with sudden fury. "This is who I am! This is the only thing that makes me MATTER!"

The stones on the table between them began to crack as Aurora's magic responded to her distress. Small tremors ran through the ground beneath their feet.

"Aurora, please calm down—"

"You want me to file this away?! Put it in a box like it's just another trauma to be managed?!" Aurora stood up abruptly, her chair falling backward. "I can't do that! If I lose this, I lose EVERYTHING!"

The tremors intensified, and Raven's carefully tended plants began to wither around the edges of the shelter. Aurora's magic was feeding on them again, her control completely shattered.

"You don't understand," Aurora continued, her voice rising. "Without that promise, I'm nothing. I've never been anything else. Every choice I've made, every sacrifice, every moment of my life has been about keeping Toby safe!"

"That's exactly why this memory needs to be organized," Raven said calmly, though Aurora could see her preparing to defend herself. "It's too powerful, too controlling. It's preventing you from making rational decisions—"

"Rational decisions?" Aurora laughed bitterly, and the sound was accompanied by a jagged crack appearing in the stone wall. "You think loving someone enough to dedicate your life to them is irrational?"

AURORA

"I think making a promise when you were six years old and never questioning it as an adult is problematic," Raven replied carefully. "Aurora, that child couldn't possibly have understood what she was agreeing to—"

"Don't you dare." Aurora's voice dropped to a dangerous whisper. "Don't you dare diminish what I promised them. They were dying, and they trusted me with the most important thing in their lives! I gave my word."

Thorny vines began erupting from the floor of the shelter, not aimed at Raven but curling protectively around Aurora herself. The message was clear: she would defend this memory, this promise, with everything she had.

"You're trying to make me forget them," Aurora accused, backing toward the shelter's entrance. "You're trying to take away the only purpose I've ever had."

"I'm trying to help you heal—"

"By betraying everything I am?" Aurora's magic lashed out again, more vines bursting through the stone walls. "By filing away the moment that made me who I am?! I won't do it. I can't."

The shelter shook as Aurora's earth magic reached its peak, undoing all of Raven's careful work. Plants died, stones cracked, and the temperature dropped as Aurora's emotional state spiraled completely out of control.

"I can't let go of the only thing that makes me matter," Aurora sobbed, collapsing to her knees among the thorny vines. "I've never been anything but Toby's protector. I don't know how to be anything else."

The destruction continued for several more minutes before Aurora's energy finally gave out. When the tremors stopped and the vines withered away, she found herself lying on the floor of the ruined shelter, sobbing into her hands.

Raven, who had weathered the magical storm with remarkable composure, looked around at the damage with mild interest rather than anger. Her memory stones were shattered, her plants were dead, and several walls had significant cracks. But she seemed more thoughtful than upset.

"Some memories aren't meant to be filed away, Aurora," she said quietly, moving to sit beside the broken woman. "Some experiences are too fundamental to who we are."

Aurora looked up at her with tear-stained eyes. "Then I can't be helped, can I? The thing that's destroying me is also the only thing that gives my life meaning."

Raven thought for a minute. Then she said, "We'll try a different approach tomorrow."

"What if there isn't one? What if this is just who I am, someone who destroys everything while trying to protect one person?"

"Then we'll figure that out too," Raven replied calmly. "But for today, you've learned something important about yourself. That's not nothing."

Aurora stared at the destruction she caused, at the ruined shelter that had been her sanctuary. "I've been that six-year-old girl my entire life," she whispered. "Trying to keep an impossible promise."

"Perhaps," Raven agreed. "But understanding that is the first step toward deciding whether that's who you want to continue being."

Aurora closed her eyes, feeling the weight of thirty years of responsibility pressing down on her. She never questioned the promise, never examined whether her interpretation of it was healthy or sustainable. She simply lived it, breathed it, become it.

And now she was faced with an impossible choice: betray the promise that defined her or continue being someone whose love caused more harm than good.

"How do I keep my promise when keeping it has made me into someone who hurts him?" she asked quietly.

Raven smiled sadly. "That, my dear, is exactly the right question to be asking."

CHAPTER FOUR:
Reluctant Partners

Hunter Diaz pulled the rental car into yet another motel parking lot, the third one they checked that morning. The gray March sky matched his mood perfectly: overcast, dreary, and promising nothing good. He glanced over at his passenger, who was staring out the window with barely concealed irritation.

"This is pointless," Odion Montgomery muttered, not bothering to look at Hunter. "She's obviously not going to be staying at some roadside motel thirty miles from Bellwater."

"You have a better idea?" Hunter asked, though his tone suggested he didn't particularly care what Odion's answer might be.

"Yeah. We could try looking in places where Aurora might realistically be hiding instead of checking every obvious location we can think of."

Hunter turned off the engine and pocketed the keys. "Well, Tobias said to check the obvious places first. So that's what we're doing."

It was a lie, and they both knew it. Tobias had said no such thing. But neither man was particularly motivated to put real effort into finding Aurora Wildwood, and checking places they knew she wouldn't be was a convenient way to waste time while technically following orders.

They walked into the motel office, a dingy little room that smelled of stale cigarettes and industrial cleaning solution. The clerk, a middle-aged woman with graying hair and suspicious eyes, looked up from her magazine.

"Help you?"

"We're looking for someone," Odion said, pulling out his phone to show her a picture of Aurora. "Tall woman, dark hair, probably would have checked in alone a few weeks ago?"

The woman squinted at the photo for exactly two seconds before shaking her head. "Nope. Haven't seen her."

"Are you sure?" Hunter pressed, though his heart wasn't in it. "Maybe she used a different name?"

"I said I haven't seen her. You want a room or not?"

"No, thank you," Odion replied quickly, already heading for the door.

They climbed back into the car in silence. Hunter started the engine but didn't immediately pull out of the parking lot. For a moment, neither man spoke.

"That makes eight motels," Odion said finally.

"Nine, if you count the one that was closed for renovations."

"Right. Nine motels, four hospitals, three hotels, and two shelters. All within a fifty-mile radius of Bellwater Academy."

Hunter drummed his fingers on the steering wheel. "Well, we're being thorough."

"We're being useless."

The truth hung in the air between them. They were going through the motions, checking boxes on an imaginary list while avoiding any real effort to locate Aurora. Hunter pulled out of the parking lot and headed toward the main road, neither man bothering to suggest their next destination.

"There's a diner up ahead," Odion said after a few more minutes of uncomfortable silence. "We should probably eat something."

Hunter nodded and pulled into the parking lot of Mel's Family Restaurant, a typical small-town establishment with faded red vinyl booths and a waitress who looked like she'd been working there since the 1980s. They slid into a booth near the back, both men immediately burying themselves in their phones to avoid conversation.

The waitress, whose name tag read "Dolores," approached with coffee without being asked. "What can I get you boys?"

They ordered quickly—Hunter a burger, Odion a club sandwich—and returned to their phones. The silence stretched on until their food arrived, broken only by the occasional clink of silverware against plates.

Finally, Hunter couldn't stand it anymore.

"You know," he said, setting down his burger and fixing Odion with a cold stare, "you've got some nerve sitting there acting all righteous about Aurora when you've known Tobias for what, a few months?"

Odion looked up from his sandwich, his eyebrows raised. "Excuse me?"

"I've known him for years. Years, Odion. I know Aurora's history, I know what she's capable of, and I know what she means to him. You're just some newcomer who thinks he understands the situation."

"Oh, I understand the situation perfectly," Odion replied, his voice dangerously quiet. "I understand that Aurora strangled a teenage girl with a sunflower because she made a sarcastic comment. I understand that she tortured a young woman for weeks trying to get information. And I understand that she killed a dozen police officers because she was too proud to surrender peacefully. I also understand that you went after the man you 'love', got him shot, then proceeded to kidnap him by exploiting his inability to not put himself before others."

Hunter's jaw tightened. "You weren't there. You don't know the context—"

Odion laughed. "No amount of 'context' excuses what either you or Aurora have done. Period. And I know that anyone who defends those actions is just as twisted as she is."

"Watch it," Hunter warned, leaning forward slightly.

"Or what?" Odion shot back. "You'll kidnap me too? Hold me prisoner for months while you play out some sick fantasy?"

The words hit Hunter like a physical blow. He felt his hands clench into fists under the table, fire magic crackling at his fingertips. Several other diners had turned to look at them, their conversation having grown loud enough to attract attention.

"I made mistakes," Hunter said through gritted teeth. "But I never—"

"You never what? Never hurt him? Never betrayed his trust? Never chose your own twisted desires over his wellbeing?"

Hunter stood up abruptly, his chair scraping loudly against the floor. The diner had gone quiet, every eye in the place fixed on their booth. Dolores was hovering nearby with the coffee pot, clearly debating whether to intervene.

"Sit down," Odion said quietly. "People are staring."

Hunter looked around, realizing for the first time they'd become the center of attention. Slowly, reluctantly, he sat back down. The conversation in the diner gradually resumed, though several patrons continued to glance in their direction.

"We can't do this," Odion said once the attention had shifted away from them. "We can't work together if we're going to be at each other's throats."

"Then maybe we should call this off," Hunter replied. "Tell Tobias we couldn't find her."

"Is that what you want? To give up?"

AURORA

Hunter stared down at his half-eaten burger. The truth was, he wasn't sure what he wanted. Part of him hoped Aurora was dead, that she finally pushed too far and paid the ultimate price for her actions. Another part of him felt guilty for thinking that way, knowing how much her loss would devastate Tobias.

"I don't know," he said finally. "Do you want to find her?"

Odion picked at his sandwich without eating it. "I keep telling myself it's my duty," he said eventually. "Tobias asked us to do this, so we should do it. But honestly? I'm not sure Aurora deserves to be found. I'm not sure the world isn't better off without her."

It was the first deeply honest thing either man had said since they started this journey, and it caught Hunter off guard. He looked up, meeting Odion's eyes for the first time in hours.

"So why are we doing this?"

"Because Tobias asked us to. And because disappointing him feels worse than working with you."

Hunter almost smiled at that. Almost. "Fair enough."

They finished their meal in relative peace, the earlier hostility replaced by a grudging understanding. Neither man was doing this because he wanted to find Aurora. They were doing it because they couldn't bear to let Tobias down.

But that didn't mean they had to like each other.

By evening, they checked three more locations—Aurora's old apartment from ten years ago, two former Bellwater safe houses, and a women's shelter in the next town over. All empty, all dead ends, all exactly what they expected to find.

The motel room they ended up sharing was a study in forced proximity and mutual discomfort. Two twin beds separated by a narrow nightstand, a bathroom barely large enough for one person, and a heater that rattled like it was preparing to die. Hunter claimed the bed nearest the door while Odion took the one by the window.

They called Tobias separately, each giving him the same disappointing update. No sign of Aurora, no promising leads, nothing but a growing list of places she wasn't. Tobias's frustration was evident even over the phone, though he tried to hide it behind encouragement and suggestions for expanding their search area.

"Keep looking," he told Hunter. "She's out there somewhere. We just need to be patient."

"Of course," Hunter had replied, though patience was the last thing on his mind.

Now they lay in their respective beds, staring at the water-stained ceiling and pretending to sleep. The silence was different from the hostile quiet that had characterized most of their day. This was the exhausted silence of two people who'd run out of energy to hate each other.

"Hunter?" Odion's voice was barely audible in the darkness.

"What?"

"Do you really think she deserves to be found?"

Hunter was quiet for so long that Odion thought he might have fallen asleep. When he finally spoke, his voice was barely a whisper.

"I don't know. Part of me hopes she's dead. Then I feel guilty for thinking that because I know it would destroy Tobias."

"Yeah," Odion agreed softly. "I know the feeling."

CHAPTER FIVE:
Unexpected Allies

The town looked the same as it had months ago when Odion had first visited with Aurora. Same rundown bar, same post office, same handful of houses scattered along the main road. Hunter pulled their rental car into the gravel parking lot outside Murphy's Tavern, the engine ticking as it cooled in the chilly March air.

"This is where you met her?" Hunter asked, staring at the weathered building.

"Yeah," Odion replied, unbuckling his seatbelt. "Aurora and I came here looking for Ted. Marina was inside, and when we started asking questions..." He trailed off, remembering the violence that had followed. The massive flood Marina had created, Aurora's brutal retaliation with the exploding roses.

"And you think Aurora might have come back here?"

Odion shrugged. "It's as good a place as any to check. Aurora knows this town exists, knows it has connections to the Rebellion. If she was desperate enough..."

They both knew it was another long shot. Aurora had no real reason to come to this town, especially not after what had happened here. But they were running out of obvious places to check, and neither man was ready to admit they should probably expand their search to less obvious locations.

The bar was dimly lit and mostly empty, just like before. The same bartender—an older man with graying hair and suspicious eyes—looked up as they entered. Odion recognized him immediately.

"Afternoon," the bartender said, though his tone suggested he remembered Odion too and wasn't particularly pleased to see them again.

"We're looking for someone," Odion said, pulling out his phone to show a picture of Aurora. "Tall woman, dark hair. Would have been alone, probably seemed... distressed."

The bartender glanced at the photo for maybe half a second before shaking his head. "Nope. Haven't seen her."

"Are you sure?" Hunter pressed.

"I said I haven't seen her." The bartender turned away, making it clear the conversation was over.

They left the bar and walked back toward their car, both men going through the motions without any real expectation of success. This was just another box to check, another dead end to report back to Tobias.

"Well, that was productive," Hunter muttered, fishing the car keys out of his pocket.

"About as productive as everything else we've done," Odion replied.

They were halfway to the car when a woman's voice called out behind them.

"Odion Montgomery."

Both men froze. The voice was familiar to them. Odion turned slowly, and his stomach dropped when he saw a blue-haired girl with deep bruises and cuts all over her body standing about twenty feet away. Marina looked different than he remembered, though he supposed not being under the threat of torture would make someone look different. Her long blue hair was pulled back in a ponytail, and she was wearing jeans and a heavy jacket against the cold. But her eyes were fixed on him with unmistakable intent.

"Marina," Odion said carefully. "What are you doing here?"

She took a step closer, and Odion noticed she was looking past him at Hunter with what appeared to be relief. "I've been waiting for you to show up here again. I figured you might come back eventually, check old leads." Her gaze shifted to Hunter, and she smiled. "Good thing you brought backup."

Hunter frowned. "Backup?"

"Hunter, help me with this guy," Marina said, her tone becoming more businesslike. "He's one of the ones who attacked our base. The Rebellion wants him for questioning."

Odion saw the exact moment when understanding dawned on Hunter's face, followed quickly by something that looked like guilt.

"Marina," Hunter said slowly, "I'm not with the Rebellion anymore."

Marina blinked. "What?"

"I left the Rebellion. I'm working with Tobias now." Hunter moved slightly, not quite stepping between Marina and Odion, but close enough to make his position clear.

Marina stared at him like he just told her the sky was purple. "That's not... Hunter, what are you talking about? You're a loyal member of the Rebellion. You wouldn't just—"

"I would, and I did." Hunter's voice was quiet but firm. "I'm sorry, Marina, but I'm not going to help you capture Odion."

The color drained from Marina's face as the implications hit her. She looked back and forth between the two men, her confident demeanor cracking.

"So you're... you're both..." She took a step backward. "You switched sides. You betrayed us."

"It's complicated," Hunter said.

"No, it's not!" Marina's voice rose, panic creeping in. "You were supposed to be my ally! You were supposed to help me, and instead I'm facing two enemies!"

She raised her hands, water beginning to swirl around her fingers. But instead of attacking, she kept backing away, her eyes darting between them like a cornered animal.

"You're going to torture me for information, aren't you?" she said, her voice shaking. "Like Aurora did to me…" She stopped herself, but the implication hung in the air.

"Marina, no," Odion said, raising his own hands in a peaceful gesture. "We're not here to hurt you."

"Right," Marina laughed bitterly. "Because Aurora's people are known for their mercy."

"We're not Aurora's people either," Hunter said quickly. "Marina, listen to me. We're not here to capture you or torture you or anything like that. We're just—"

"Looking for Aurora," Odion finished.

Marina stopped backing away, confusion replacing some of the fear in her eyes. "Looking for Aurora? Why would you want to find her?"

Hunter and Odion exchanged a glance. How did they explain that Tobias had asked them to find Aurora, but they'd been half-heartedly going through the motions because neither of them wanted to succeed?

"Tobias asked us to," Odion said finally. "She disappeared a few weeks ago, and he's… concerned."

"Concerned," Marina repeated flatly. "About Aurora Wildwood. The woman who killed a dozen police officers and strangled a teenage girl with a sunflower."

"Like I said, it's complicated," Hunter muttered.

Marina studied their faces, looking for signs of deception. Slowly, the water around her hands began to settle.

"You're serious," she said. "You're actually looking for her."

"Unfortunately, yes," Odion replied.

"And you're not trying to capture me for the Rebellion."

"No," both men said simultaneously.

Marina processed this information. When she spoke again, her voice was calmer but still wary.

"How's that search going for you?"

Hunter grimaced. "Not great."

"We've been checking obvious places," Odion admitted. "Motels, hospitals, that sort of thing."

"Finding anything?"

"No," Hunter said. "Nothing."

Marina nodded slowly. "That's because you're looking in all the wrong places. Aurora's not going to check into a motel under her own name. If she's having some kind of breakdown—which, let's be honest, was probably inevitable—she'd go somewhere remote. Somewhere she could lose control without witnesses."

"You seem to know a lot about her breakdown patterns," Odion observed.

"I know Aurora's reputation in the Rebellion. Powerful but unstable. The kind of person you don't want to be around when she snaps." Marina crossed her arms. "If she's really lost it completely, she's dangerous. Not just to herself, but to anyone who gets in her way."

"So?" Hunter asked.

Marina was quiet again, clearly wrestling with something. Finally, she sighed.

"So I'm going to help you find her."

Both men stared at her. "You're what?" Odion asked.

"I'm going to help you find Aurora," Marina repeated. "Not because I like either of you, and definitely not because I care what happens to her. But because if Aurora's out there having a magical meltdown, innocent people are going to get hurt. And I've seen enough people get hurt because of that woman."

"Why would you want to help us?" Hunter asked suspiciously. "You just found out I betrayed the Rebellion. You have every reason to hate both of us."

"I do hate both of you," Marina said matter-of-factly. "You attacked our base," she pointed at Odion, "and you're a traitor," she pointed at Hunter. "But this is bigger than my personal feelings. Aurora needs to be stopped before she kills someone else."

Odion and Hunter looked at each other, having a silent conversation. Finally, Hunter shrugged.

"We could use the help," he admitted. "We haven't exactly been... thorough in our search."

"Yeah, I figured that out," Marina said dryly. "You two have been going through the motions, haven't you? Checking places you know she won't be, so you can tell Tobias you tried."

The accuracy of her assessment was uncomfortable. Neither man bothered to deny it.

"So, what do you suggest?" Odion asked.

Marina pulled out a small notebook from her jacket pocket. "I

AURORA

know where the Rebellion keeps safe houses. Remote locations, off the grid, the kind of places someone could hide if they wanted to disappear. If Aurora's smart—and crazy as she is, she's still smart—she'd avoid anywhere connected to Bellwater. But she might use Rebellion resources if she's desperate enough."

She flipped through a few pages, then looked up at them.

"There are three locations within driving distance that fit the profile. Isolated, defensible, stocked with supplies. If Aurora's having a breakdown and needs somewhere to hide, one of these places would be perfect."

"And you're willing to take us there?" Hunter asked.

"I'm willing to take you to check them out," Marina corrected. "But let's be clear about something. This is a temporary partnership. I don't trust either of you, I don't like either of you, and once we find Aurora, we go our separate ways. Understood?"

"Understood," Odion said.

"Good." Marina closed the notebook and headed toward their car. "Let's go find your missing psychopath before she hurts someone else."

As they walked, Hunter fell into step beside Odion.

"Think we can trust her?" Hunter asked quietly.

Odion watched Marina's determined stride, remembering the fear in her eyes when she thought they were going to torture her.

"I think she wants to find Aurora even more than Tobias does," he replied. "Just for very different reasons."

They climbed into the car—Marina claiming the back seat—and for the first time since they'd started this search, they had an actual plan. It wasn't friendship that brought them together, and it certainly wasn't forgiveness. But sometimes, shared purpose was enough.

CHAPTER SIX:
Administrative Pressure

The rain drummed against the windows of Tobias's office with the persistence of someone who wouldn't take no for an answer. Much like everything else in his life these days, he thought grimly as he stared at the stack of paperwork threatening to topple off his desk. Substitute teacher requests. Incident reports. Budget forms that made absolutely no sense. Parent complaint letters that grew more aggressive with each passing day.

Tobias rubbed his temples and reached for his coffee mug, only to discover it was empty. Again. The bitter dregs at the bottom had gone cold hours ago, but he'd been too buried in administrative hell to notice. When had he last eaten? Yesterday? The day before? Time had become a meaningless concept since Aurora disappeared weeks ago, leaving him to somehow explain away the exodus of half their teaching staff.

The phone rang. Again.

"Mr. Thornfield?" Beatrice's voice crackled through the ancient telephony system. "Dr. Harrington from the state is here to see you. She says it's urgent."

Tobias's blood turned to ice. Dr. Harrington? He wasn't expecting any visit from the state. His mind raced through everything that could have triggered this level of attention—missing teachers, incident reports, the earthquake that had conveniently killed half the local police force. Though how the state could possibly tie that back to the teachers of Bellwater Academy, Tobias had no idea.

"Send her in," he managed to say, though his voice came out as more of a croak.

He frantically shuffled papers, trying to make his desk look less like a disaster zone and more like something a competent administrator might manage. The effort was pointless. His office looked exactly like what it was: the workspace of a man drowning in responsibilities he'd never wanted and wasn't qualified for.

The door opened, and Dr. Patricia Harrington entered like she owned the place. Mid-fifties, impeccably dressed in a charcoal gray suit that probably cost more than Tobias made in a month. She carried a thick manila folder that looked ominous enough to contain his death warrant.

"Mr. Thornfield." She sat down across from him without being invited, placing the folder on his desk with deliberate precision. "Thank you for seeing me on such short notice."

"Of course," Tobias replied, biting down the "like I had a choice" retort that came to him almost at once. "How can I help you today?"

Dr. Harrington opened her folder and removed a stack of documents. "We have some…concerns…about the leadership situation here at Bellwater Academy. I understand Principal Percival Ion died several months ago. He was replaced by Aurora Wildwood, who was the Guidance Counselor. And now…you. Let's start with your recent appointment as interim principal. Quite a rapid career advancement, wouldn't you say?"

"I suppose it was unexpected, yes."

"Unexpected." She made a note on her pad. "According to my

records, you were terminated from a substitute teaching position at this very school just weeks before being appointed to run it. Care to explain how that worked?"

Tobias felt sweat gathering at the back of his neck despite the cool March air. "There were...circumstances surrounding Principal Ion's departure. The school board felt I was familiar with the staff and students, so—"

"Principal Ion." Dr. Harrington consulted her papers. "Who died in what witnesses described as a gas explosion, though there's no record of any gas leak repairs or utility company investigations."

"I wasn't involved in the investigation of that incident."

"No, of course not." Her smile was razor-thin. "Let's move on to staffing. This school has lost nearly half its teaching staff in two months. That's unprecedented in state records."

Tobias opened his mouth, but she continued before he could speak.

"Ms. Aurora Wildwood, the former guidance counselor, now the former interim principal. Her departure wasn't properly documented. No forwarding address, no transition plans, no explanation beyond 'personal emergency.' Where exactly is Ms. Wildwood?"

"She had a family crisis that required her immediate attention—"

"What kind of family crisis?"

"I...I'm not privy to the personal details—"

"Mr. Montgomery. Math teacher. Also departed with minimal notice." Dr. Harrington was reading from her notes now, her voice taking on the mechanical quality of someone reciting an indictment. "Ms. Braithwaite, science teacher. Mr. Rodson, art and music. All gone within weeks of each other. All with vague explanations about personal matters or family emergencies."

Each name felt like a physical blow. Tobias tried to maintain eye contact, but her stare was relentless.

"Dr. Harrington, teaching is a demanding profession. Sometimes personal circumstances—"

"Mr. Thornfield." She leaned forward. "I've been investigating troubled schools for fifteen years. I've seen budget crises, administrative incompetence, even corruption. But I've never seen a pattern quite like this."

She pulled out another set of documents. "Let's discuss the incidents. The earthquake that damaged several buildings in town, including significant structural damage to this school. Yet there are no insurance claims filed, no repair orders, no geological survey reports."

"The damage was mostly cosmetic—"

"Twelve police officers died in that earthquake, Mr. Thornfield. The entire downtown area was affected. But your school, which allegedly suffered structural damage, somehow continued operating without any safety inspections or repairs."

Tobias felt the walls closing in. "I'm not an expert on building codes—"

"Then there are the gas leaks. Three in two weeks. Electrical problems that required evacuating students. Water main breaks in the basement that flooded the lower level." Dr. Harrington's voice grew sharper with each item. "These incidents cluster around your school in a statistically impossible pattern."

"Old building," Tobias offered weakly. "Sometimes problems come in waves."

"Sometimes." She closed the folder with a snap that made Tobias flinch. "Or sometimes there are other explanations."

The silence stretched between them like a taut wire. Rain continued to pelt the windows, and somewhere in the building, a door slammed. Normal school sounds that felt completely alien in the context of this conversation.

Just as Dr. Harrington opened her mouth to continue, the office door burst open.

"Mr. T! Ready for today's lesson? I've been practicing the lightning exercises you showed me—"

Foxton Gray stood in the doorway, bright-faced and eager, completely oblivious to the formal meeting in progress. His red hair was damp from the rain, and his backpack was slung over one shoulder like he was ready for adventure.

The world stopped.

Dr. Harrington's head snapped toward Foxton with predatory interest. "Lightning exercises?"

Tobias felt his entire body go cold. "Foxton, not now! This is not the time!"

The harshness in his own voice surprised him. Foxton's face fell like Tobias had slapped him.

"But Mr. T, you said—"

"I'm in an important meeting. You need to leave. Now." Tobias gestured sharply toward the door, his panic making him cruder than he'd ever been with a student. "We'll discuss your...activities...later."

Foxton's confusion was painful to see. The boy who trusted him implicitly, who looked up to him, who called him Mr. T with such genuine affection, stood there looking like he'd been betrayed by his best friend.

"But I thought—"

"Out, Foxton!"

The boy left, but not before Tobias saw the hurt in his eyes. The door closed with a soft click that somehow sounded louder than if it had been slammed.

"Interesting relationship with your students, Mr. Thornfield." Dr. Harrington's pen was poised over her notepad. "What kind of lessons and exercises occur after hours? And why is the principal personally offering these lessons instead of a classroom teacher?"

"Tutoring," Tobias said quickly. "Academic support for struggling students."

"Lightning exercises for academic support."

"It's…a metaphor. For quick thinking. Brain exercises."

Dr. Harrington's expression suggested she found his explanation about as convincing as a three-dollar bill. She made several notes, her pen scratching across the paper like fingernails on a chalkboard.

"Mr. Thornfield, I've seen enough." She closed her notepad with finality. "This requires a full state investigation."

The words hit him like a physical blow. "Dr. Harrington, surely that's not necessary—"

"Too many irregularities. Too many missing pieces. Too many questions without satisfactory answers." She stood up, smoothing her skirt. "Your school will be placed under state oversight effective immediately."

Tobias's mouth went dry. "What does that mean?"

"It means a team of investigators will arrive within forty-eight hours. Staff interviews will be mandatory and conducted separately. Student interviews, including these transfer students with questionable records." She gestured toward where Foxton had been standing. "Financial audit of all school accounts. Background checks on all personnel."

"Dr. Harrington, please. The students have been through enough trauma. They lost their families in that fire—"

"Which is exactly why we need to ensure their safety." Her voice softened slightly, but her eyes remained steel. "Any interference with this investigation will result in immediate school closure."

School closure. The words echoed in Tobias's head like a death knell. Without the school, they had no cover. No legitimate reason for their community to exist. No way to protect the magical students.

"You have until my team arrives to produce documentation for every missing staff member," Dr. Harrington continued. "Satisfactory explanations for every incident report. And I want a complete list of all after-hours activities involving students."

"Forty-eight hours?"

"Forty-eight hours." She picked up her folder and headed for the door. "I suggest you use them wisely, Mr. Thornfield."

The door closed behind her with a decisive click, leaving Tobias alone with the magnitude of what had just happened. He slumped back in his chair, staring at the ceiling tiles that were probably older than he was.

Forty-eight hours to explain the unexplainable. To produce missing people who were either in hiding or had defected to the enemy. To somehow make a magical crisis look like routine administrative chaos.

He needed to call someone. But who? Aurora was missing. Odion, Sabrina, Lucien, all gone. Agatha was recovering from her hip injury and wouldn't be much help even if she were available.

The phone rang again, but he didn't answer it. Outside, the rain continued its relentless assault on the windows, as if the weather itself was conspiring against him.

A soft knock interrupted his spiraling thoughts.

"Mr. T?" Foxton's voice was tentative through the door. "Are you okay? I'm sorry I interrupted, I just..."

Tobias stared at the door, his heart breaking a little more. Foxton was probably the one person left who still trusted him completely, and he'd just thrown that trust back in the boy's face. But how could he explain? How could he apologize without revealing everything they'd worked so hard to hide?

"Come in, Foxton."

The boy entered cautiously, like he was approaching a wounded animal. "I really didn't mean to mess up your meeting. I know you've been stressed, and—"

"It's not your fault," Tobias said quietly. "It's mine. All of it."

Foxton moved closer to the desk, concern written across his freckled face. "What's happening, Mr. T? Everyone's been acting weird lately. People disappearing, meetings getting canceled, and now that lady in the suit..."

Tobias looked at this boy who'd lost everything—his family, his friends, his entire world—and had somehow maintained enough faith to keep trusting the adults around him. How long before that trust was completely shattered?

"I can't explain everything right now, Foxton. But I need you to know that whatever happens in the next few days, whatever questions people ask you, whatever they want to know about our training sessions..."

He paused, trying to find words that would convey urgency without revealing too much.

"Be careful what you say. Some things are better kept between us."

Foxton's eyes widened with understanding that went beyond his years. "Are we in trouble?"

"I don't know yet," Tobias admitted. "But I'm going to do everything I can to protect you and Finnian. All of you."

It was a promise he had no idea how to keep. But looking at Foxton's trusting face, he knew he'd find a way or die trying.

CHAPTER SEVEN:
What Really Matters

Tobias sat alone in his office, staring at the stack of papers Dr. Harrington had left behind like a death sentence. The demands were impossible: detailed personnel files for missing staff members, incident reports for "irregularities" he couldn't begin to explain, documentation for policies that existed only in the magical world she would never understand.

How do you explain the unexplainable?

He picked up the first form: a request for employment verification for Sabrina Braithwaite. The woman who had betrayed them all, who was probably plotting their destruction at this very moment, and the state wanted her W-2 forms. The absurdity of it would have been funny if it weren't so terrifying.

His phone sat on the desk, and for a moment he considered calling Odion. Odion would know what to do; he was practical, resourceful, and Tobias trusted him completely. But calling Odion would mean exposing him to danger, dragging him back into a mess that could destroy whatever peaceful life he might be building.

Then there was Hunter. Hunter could solve this with a snap of his fingers, forge documents, manipulate records, make Dr. Harrington believe whatever story they needed her to believe. But at what cost? How many more innocent people would suffer for their convenience?

Tobias pushed the papers away and put his head in his hands. "I won't drag anyone else down with me," he said aloud to the empty office.

The realization hit him like a physical blow: Bellwater Academy might be lost. All of it. The school, the cover for their magical operations, the haven they'd built for students like Foxton and Finnian. Maybe no amount of paperwork could fix this. Maybe some things, once broken, couldn't be repaired.

A knock on his door interrupted his spiral into despair. "Come in," he called, straightening the papers he'd scattered.

Matilda poked her head in, followed by Agatha on her crutches and Beatrice from the front office. The three women looked as grim as he felt.

"We need to talk," Agatha said without preamble, settling herself into one of the chairs with obvious effort. "All of us."

They moved to the small conference room near the main office. Tobias closed the door and looked at the three women who represented what was left of Bellwater Academy's staff. Loyal, hardworking, two of them aware of the magical storm surrounding them. Beatrice left in the dark.

"State investigators will be here in forty-six hours," he began. "They'll interview all of us separately. They'll want answers I can't give them."

"About what exactly?" Matilda asked, though her tone suggested she already suspected.

"Missing staff members. The teachers who left without proper notice, without forwarding addresses, without explanations." Agatha and Matilda knew about Sabrina's betrayal, about Lucien's defection to the Arcane Rebellion, about Aurora's disappearance. But he dared not say anything more in front of Beatrice, who was not a mage. "Personal emergencies, family crises. Things happened quickly."

Agatha studied him with sharp eyes. "They're going to shut us down, aren't they?"

The blunt question hit the room like a slap. Tobias had been dancing around it, but Agatha had always preferred the truth to comfortable lies.

"Probably," he admitted. "I'm sorry. This is my fault."

"What do we tell them about the missing teachers?" Matilda pressed.

"The truth, as you said. Personal emergencies, family crises. Don't volunteer information, but don't lie."

Beatrice shifted in her chair, her beady eyes narrowed. "What about the students? The transfer students especially?"

Those words hit Tobias in the chest. The transfer students, the survivors from Jefferson High who had lost everything and trusted Bellwater Academy to give them a new start. Foxton and Finnian, who called him Mr. T and looked to him for guidance. The other kids scattered throughout the building who had nowhere else to go.

"Protect them," he said firmly. "That's all that matters now."

The women exchanged glances, and Agatha leaned forward on her crutches. "We'll get through this, Tobias. One way or another."

They talked for another twenty minutes, going over basic protocols, agreeing not to coordinate their stories beyond the simple truth. When they finally left, Tobias felt marginally better. Not because the problem was solved, but because he remembered he wasn't facing it alone.

As he walked back toward his office, he heard familiar voices in the hallway. Foxton and Finnian were outside the conference room, clearly having waited through the entire meeting.

"He didn't mean it, Fox," Finnian was saying quietly. "Something's really wrong."

"I know," Foxton replied, his voice tight with worry. "That's what scares me. What if we lose him too?"

Tobias stopped in the shadows, watching the two boys walk away together. Foxton's arm was around Finnian's shoulders—natural leadership, protective instincts, the kind of loyalty that couldn't be taught. Finnian's steady presence, the quiet intelligence that asked the right questions at the right times.

These were the kids he'd thought were worth saving when he'd first met them at Jefferson High. When had he stopped trusting them? When had he started seeing them as problems to manage instead of people worth protecting?

The rain was still falling when Tobias left the school building two hours later. Instead of heading back to Aurora's cottage, he found himself walking through the village toward the safe house where Foxton and Finnian lived. Each step felt heavier than the last, not from exhaustion but from the weight of what he needed to do.

He stood outside their door for a full minute before knocking, water dripping from his hair. When Foxton answered, his eyes widened in surprise.

"Mr. T? What are you doing here?"

"Can we talk? All three of us?"

They sat around the small kitchen table that dominated their modest living space. The awkwardness was palpable. Tobias still owed Foxton an apology, and they all knew it.

"I owe you both an apology," he began, "but especially you, Foxton." He looked directly at the red-haired boy whose trust he'd broken. "I was scared, and I took it out on you. That was wrong. You've both been through enough without your teacher failing you too."

Foxton's expression softened slightly, but he didn't speak.

"The school is in trouble," Tobias continued. "The state thinks we've been... irregular. They're going to investigate everything. Interview everyone. I can't tell you everything, but I need you to know this isn't about anything you did wrong."

Finnian, ever the analytical one, spoke first. "It's about the people who left, isn't it?"

"Are we going to lose the school too, Mr. T?" Foxton asked directly.

Tobias appreciated that, no dancing around the hard questions. "I don't know. Maybe."

The boys absorbed this information with maturity that broke his heart. Instead of panicking about their own situation, their first concern was for others.

"What about the other kids?" Foxton asked. "The ones who lost their families?"

"What can we do to help?" Finnian added.

And there it was, the reason Tobias had seen potential in them from the beginning. In the face of loss, their instinct was to help others.

After a moment, Foxton's expression grew more serious. "What about Sabrina and Lucien? You said we needed to find them, that they were dangerous."

Tobias felt a flicker of pride. Despite everything, Foxton was still thinking about their larger mission, still remembering the threats that existed beyond the mundane crisis of the investigation.

"You're right. They are still out there, and they are still dangerous," Tobias acknowledged. "But right now, if we don't handle this investigation properly, there won't be a school left to protect anyone from. We need to secure our foundation before we can go after them."

Finnian nodded slowly. "So, we're playing defense first, then offense?"

"Exactly. Once the investigators are satisfied or gone, then we'll focus on Sabrina and Lucien. But if we're exposed now, if the school is shut down, we lose our cover and our ability to help anyone."

"Okay," Foxton said, "but we don't forget about them, right?"

"We don't forget. But we're patient."

Tobias leaned forward. "When they interview you, be careful what you say about our training sessions. Remember: magic is best kept a secret. Better to have them believe we're doing extra academic tutoring or something. Can I trust you both with that?"

Both boys nodded immediately.

"We've got your back, Mr. T," Foxton said. "Always have."

"What do you need us to do?" Finnian asked.

They spent the next hour working together, not coaching lies but helping the boys prepare for difficult questions. "They'll ask about lightning exercises, Fox. What will you say?" They worked out honest but careful responses, making sure their stories would align without being fabricated.

As they talked, Tobias realized something had shifted. The boys weren't just students anymore; they were partners, allies who understood that there were adult complexities beyond their full comprehension but who were ready to stand with him anyway.

By the time he left their house, the rain had grown heavier, but Tobias felt lighter than he had all day. He'd spent the entire afternoon not working on Dr. Harrington's impossible demands, not filling out forms or creating documentation that couldn't possibly satisfy the investigation.

But he'd accomplished something more important. He'd remembered what was worth protecting.

CHAPTER EIGHT:
The Weight of a Promise

Aurora lay crumpled on the floor of what remained of Raven's shelter, her body trembling uncontrollably. The magical and emotional release had left her completely drained, as though something fundamental had been ripped from her very core. Small tremors continued to ripple through the earth beneath her, her magic still responding to the devastating realization that had torn through her consciousness.

"I promised them," she whispered, her voice barely audible above the storm raging outside. "I promised his parents I'd keep him safe."

The memory hung in the air like a physical weight. Aurora could still see herself as a tiny six-year-old, standing in her own living room beside that makeshift deathbed. She could still feel the desperation in Tobias's parents' eyes; the absolute trust they had placed in her when they had no one else to turn to.

Raven knelt beside her, offering a steady hand that Aurora was too weak to refuse. "Tell me about this promise," she said gently.

Aurora tried to sit up but couldn't manage it without support. Every part of her felt hollow, scraped clean by the force of the recovered memory. "They were dying," she said in broken fragments. "His parents.

AURORA

They had brought him to our house because they knew my grandmother could help magical children. They were so sick, and Tobias...he was just a baby. Only two years old."

She trailed off, overwhelmed by the weight of what she was remembering. "They asked me to take care of him. A six-year-old girl, and they were begging me to watch over their toddler son. 'He has no one else,' they said. And I...I gave my word. I swore I would protect him."

The words came out like a confession, each one carrying the burden of years of failure. Aurora pressed her palms against the floor, feeling the earth respond to her anguish with subtle shaking.

"I thought I was protecting him," she continued, her voice growing stronger with desperation. "Everything I did, every decision I made was all about keeping him safe. But look what I've done." The tremors intensified. "I've driven him away. Made his life more dangerous. Nearly got him killed with my own inability to control myself."

Raven listened without judgment, her weathered face reflecting understanding rather than condemnation. "You were six years old when you made that promise," she observed.

"That doesn't matter!" Aurora snapped, then immediately winced as the earth cracked beneath her hands. "I gave my word. To dying parents. The most sacred kind of trust there is. And I failed. Everything I've done has pushed him away from me instead of protecting him."

She began cataloging her failures with the methodical precision of someone who had been carrying this guilt for years. "The police massacre—how many enemies did that create for him? The way I attacked that student, lost control...what kind of example was I setting? What kind of danger was I putting him in just by being near him?"

The memories came flooding back now: every time her fierce protection had become control, every instance where she needed to shield Tobias from harm had created more problems. The realization was crushing.

"He could have died because of me," she whispered. "Because I couldn't keep myself together when he needed me to be stable. The one person I swore to protect, and I made his life worse."

Raven shifted closer, choosing her words carefully. "Tell me about when you made this promise. Help me understand what it meant to you."

Aurora closed her eyes, and the memory played out with painful clarity. "They had come to our house seeking help. Tobias's parents were so sick; some kind of magical drain that was killing them slowly."

She could see it all again: her parents' living room, the makeshift bed they'd set up, little Tobias toddling around while his parents grew weaker by the hour. "My mother was trying to help them, but it was too late. They knew they were dying. And they...they looked at me, this little girl, and asked me to promise to take care of their son."

The weight of that moment crashed over her again. "I didn't understand what I was promising, not really. I was six. But I looked them in the eyes and swore I would. It felt like the most important thing I'd ever said. Like my entire purpose in life was suddenly clear."

"And it shaped everything after that," Raven said, not a question but an understanding.

"Everything," Aurora confirmed. "Every threat to Tobias felt like a personal failure. Every time he got hurt or was in danger, it was like I was breaking my word all over again. I had to control everything around him to keep him safe, because if something happened to him..." She shuddered. "I couldn't bear to face their memory knowing I'd failed."

Raven pondered her next words for a long time, and when she spoke, her voice carried the weight of her own experiences. "I tried to protect my son by controlling everything around him too," she said carefully. "Good intentions can become harmful actions, especially when we're carrying that kind of responsibility."

AURORA

Aurora's head snapped up, her eyes flashing with defensive anger. The earth responded, tremors increasing in intensity. "You don't understand. This isn't about good intentions going wrong. This is about a sacred promise to dying parents, and I broke it. I failed completely."

"How did you fail?" Raven asked, her voice remaining calm despite the magical instability building around them.

"Are you serious?" Aurora's voice rose, and several small cracks appeared in the floor. "Look at everything I've done! The violence, the loss of control, driving him away when he needed me most. I was supposed to keep him safe, and instead I made myself into one of the dangers he needed protection from."

She pushed herself partially upright, her magic crackling with her emotional state. "If I can't keep one promise, the most important promise I've ever made, what good am I? What kind of person does that make me?!"

The fear underneath her anger was becoming clear now: the terror that she was fundamentally untrustworthy, that her failure meant she was beyond redemption. "Maybe he's better off without me," she whispered. "Maybe I should just stay away forever."

Raven moved closer, speaking with quiet intensity that cut through Aurora's spiral. "What do you think Tobias's parents would want for him now?"

The question stopped Aurora cold. She stared at Raven, her magical output stuttering.

"Think about it," Raven continued. "Would they want him to carry the burden of your self-hatred? Would they want him to lose someone he cares about because you're too focused on your own guilt to be there for him?"

Aurora opened her mouth to argue, then closed it. The realization hit her like a physical blow. "Even now," she said slowly, "I'm making this about me. About my failure, my guilt, my suffering. Instead of thinking about what he needs."

"And what does he need?" Raven prompted gently.

The two women were silent for a long time, the tremors in the earth gradually subsiding as Aurora thought. "He needs...he needs someone he can trust. Someone stable, who won't hurt him or the people he cares about. Someone who will support him instead of trying to control him."

"Can you be that person?"

"I don't know," Aurora admitted. "I don't know if I can change enough to be worthy of the trust his parents placed in me. But..." She paused, something shifting in her expression. "Maybe that's exactly what I need to figure out. Maybe the best way to honor their memory and protect him now is to fix what's broken in me."

The storm outside was beginning to calm, and Aurora's magic was finally stabilizing. For the first time since the memory had returned, she felt something other than despair: purpose.

"I can't undo what I've done," she said, her voice growing stronger. "I can't take back the violence or the control or the times I failed him. But I can make sure I don't do it again. I can become someone worthy of his trust again."

Raven nodded approvingly. "Now you're thinking like someone who truly loves him."

Aurora looked at her hands, no longer trembling. "The promise isn't broken unless I give up on him completely. And I won't do that. I'll do whatever work is necessary to become the person I should have been all along."

She met Raven's eyes with new determination. "When I see him again—and I will see him again—I want to be someone he can rely on. Someone who protects him by being healthy and stable, not by trying to control his world."

"That's a worthy goal," Raven said. "And it's going to be hard work."

"Good," Aurora replied firmly. "He deserves someone who's willing to do hard work for him. His parents trusted me to help him become who he's meant to be. I can still do that. I just have to become who I'm meant to be first."

As Aurora settled into sleep that night, the shelter finally quieted around them, she felt something she hadn't experienced in months, years maybe: clarity of purpose. The guilt was still there, and probably always would be. But now it had direction. She would heal not for absolution, but for effectiveness. She would become someone worthy of the trust that had been placed in her so many years ago.

"If I truly love him," she whispered to herself as sleep took her, "I'll do the work."

CHAPTER NINE:
Learning to Remember

Aurora woke to sunlight filtering through the gaps in Raven's rebuilt shelter. The earth beneath her felt stable, solid; not the trembling, uncertain ground that had become her constant companion. Around the shelter, she could see small green weeds pushing through the soil where yesterday there had been only withered decay.

I know what I need to do now, she thought, stretching carefully. *The hard part is over.*

Her magic hummed quietly, controlled and purposeful. Plants responded to her presence with growth rather than death. She had found her anchor in the promise to protect Tobias, and it felt like everything had clicked into place.

"I thought I was better," she whispered to herself, sitting up with more energy than she'd felt in weeks.

Then, without warning, the memory hit her like a physical blow.

Tobias collapsing in the alleyway, blood spreading across his shirt. The sound of the gunshot echoing off the buildings. Her helplessness as Odion carried him away, not knowing if he would live or die.

The earth cracked beneath her with a sharp snap. The tender weeds around the shelter withered instantly, curling black at the edges. Aurora gasped, scrambling backward as her magic lashed out uncontrolled.

"No, no, no!" she cried, pressing her hands to her temples. "I thought I was better!"

"Purpose is the beginning, not the end," Raven's calm voice came from the shelter's entrance. The older woman stepped outside, surveying the fresh damage with an expression of mild interest rather than surprise. "Now we do the real work."

Aurora stared at the destruction she had caused in mere seconds—the cracked earth, the dead plants, the way even the morning air seemed to recoil from her presence. Her brief moment of hope crumbled like ash.

"You can't think your way out of trauma responses," Raven continued, settling onto a fallen log nearby. "Having a purpose is wonderful, Aurora. But your mind doesn't know the difference between memory and reality. When that memory hit you, your body believed Tobias was being shot all over again."

Aurora surveyed the damage more carefully, cataloging each withered plant, each crack in the earth. "How can I promise to be better if I can't control this? Look what I did in one moment!"

"Control isn't the goal," Raven replied firmly. "Management is."

Aurora turned to face her, confusion evident on her face.

"Your memories are scattered throughout your mind like loose papers," Raven explained, her voice taking on the patient tone of a teacher. "Traumatic memories are mixing with your daily thoughts, triggering constant magical responses. Every time you think about what you need to do today, your mind stumbles across the image of Tobias bleeding in that alley."

"I don't want to forget what I've done," Aurora said quickly. "I need to remember so I don't repeat it."

"Organization isn't erasure," Raven assured her. "It's filing. You'll still have access to every memory; they just won't control you anymore."

Aurora frowned, trying to understand. "What do you mean?"

"Think of it this way," Raven said, picking up a handful of soil and letting it run through her fingers. "Right now, your important memories are scattered on the floor of your mind. Every time you try to walk through your thoughts, you trip over them. We need to organize them, so they don't ambush you."

"But what if I need to remember something quickly? What if I need those lessons to make better choices?"

"You'll be able to find them when you need them," Raven explained patiently. "But they won't be able to find you. The difference between a memory ambushing you and you choosing to remember something is the difference between being attacked and being in control."

Inside the shelter, Raven had Aurora sit cross-legged on a woven mat. "We'll start small," she said, settling across from her. "Choose a minor upsetting memory to practice with. Something that bothers you but won't overwhelm you."

Aurora thought. "The moment I realized Percival was working against us. When I understood he'd been undermining me for months."

"Good. That's painful but manageable," Raven nodded. "Now, I want you to think about that memory clearly. Don't fight the feelings that come with it."

Aurora closed her eyes and let herself remember. The disappointment, the sense of betrayal, the way it had made her question her own judgment. She felt her magic respond slightly, the earth beneath her shifting almost imperceptibly.

"Now," Raven's voice was steady and calm, "I want you to imagine that memory as a physical object. What does it look like?"

"I still don't understand what you mean."

"If that memory were something you could hold in your hands, what would it be? A photograph? A letter? A stone?"

Aurora concentrated, trying to visualize. "A crumpled piece of paper, I think. With angry scribbles on it."

"Perfect. Now imagine placing that crumpled paper in a labeled folder. You're not destroying it, you're organizing it. The folder might be labeled 'Betrayals at Work' or 'Lessons About Trust.' Whatever feels right to you."

Aurora tried to visualize the process, but the memory kept slipping away from her mental grasp like water through her fingers. Every time she thought she had it contained, it would escape and flood her thoughts again.

"This is harder than it sounds," she muttered, frustration creeping into her voice. Her magic responded to the irritation, requiring her to take deep breaths to keep it stable.

"Of course it's hard," Raven said calmly. "Your mind has been organizing memories randomly for months. We're teaching it a new system."

After several attempts and frequent breaks, Aurora finally managed to hold the visualization for a few minutes. The relief was immediate; the memory of Percival's betrayal was still there, but it wasn't intruding on her other thoughts.

"I can still remember it if I want to," she said with wonder, "but it's not bothering me."

"Exactly," Raven smiled. "It's like organizing a messy room. Everything is still there, but now you can find what you need without tripping over everything else."

By late afternoon, Aurora was feeling more confident. "I want to try something bigger," she announced. "The police massacre. If I can organize that memory, I'll be so much better."

Raven held up a cautionary hand. "We need to work up to the big ones, Aurora. That's one of your heaviest traumatic memories."

"But I'm ready," Aurora insisted. "I understand the process now."

Before Raven could stop her, Aurora dove into the memory. The alleyway, the guns pointed at her, the earth trembling with her rage, the bodies scattered afterward. The full weight of what she had done crashed over her like a tidal wave.

The earth around the shelter bucked and cracked. Plants withered in a rapidly expanding circle. Aurora's breathing became ragged as the memory fought back, refusing to be contained.

"Come back to the present," Raven's voice cut through the chaos. "Feel the earth beneath you, Aurora. The memory is not happening now. You are safe."

Gradually, Aurora's magic calmed. The trembling stopped. She found herself gasping, tears streaming down her face.

"Trauma memories have more weight," Raven explained gently. "They need more preparation. We don't try to lift the heaviest weight on our first day at the gym."

Aurora wiped her eyes, frustration evident in every line of her body. "I want to be better for him now, not months from now."

That evening, both women sat outside the shelter, exhausted from the day's work. Aurora stared at the stars beginning to appear in the darkening sky.

"How long will this take?" she asked quietly. "What if Tobias needs me? What if I'm too broken to fix?"

"Healing isn't about speed," Raven replied. "It's about thoroughness. Would you rather be ready in six months, or need to start over in six weeks because you rushed the process?"

Aurora considered this. "I want to do it right," she said finally. "If I truly want to protect him, I need to be stable, not just sorry."

"The people we love deserve our best effort, not our fastest effort," Raven agreed.

CHAPTER TEN:
One Memory at a Time

Aurora woke to sunlight streaming through the windows of Raven's mountain shelter. The crisp mountain air carried a sense of clarity that seemed to match something inside her, a quiet resolve that felt different from the desperate determination of previous days. For the first time in weeks, her magic felt stable. She could see it in the plants around the shelter, which showed healthy growth instead of the chaotic spurts and withering that had marked her emotional turmoil.

"Today I'm ready to do the real work," she murmured to herself, stretching and feeling the truth of those words settle into her bones.

Raven was already awake, sitting by the window with her tea, observing Aurora with cautious optimism. "Your stability has improved significantly," she noted, her voice carrying the careful tone of a healer who had seen too many false dawns. "The memory barriers are holding well."

Aurora nodded, surprised by how grounded she felt. "Purpose has given me an anchor," she said, echoing something Raven had told her days ago. "Now we build the skills."

"Exactly." Raven set down her cup and studied Aurora carefully. "I think you're ready for something more challenging than yesterday's small memory. We need something significant but manageable. A memory with weight, but one where you succeeded."

Aurora's mind immediately went to a specific place, a specific moment. "When I saved Tobias," she said without hesitation.

Raven raised an eyebrow. "Tell me about a time you fulfilled your promise successfully."

Aurora was quiet for a moment, several options surfacing in her mind; times she'd protected Tobias from physical danger, moments she'd provided emotional support during his darkest periods. But one stood out with crystal clarity. "The boulder incident at Bellwater Clearing," she said slowly. "I almost lost him that day. If I'd been even a minute later…"

"Success memories can still carry trauma," Raven warned gently. "Sometimes our victories are the heaviest memories of all."

Aurora felt her magic respond to the anticipation, energy building under her skin, but it felt manageable rather than overwhelming. "I understand," she said. "This isn't about filing away shame. It's about organizing overwhelming responsibility, isn't it?"

"Precisely." Raven gestured for Aurora to sit cross-legged on the floor. "Success memories need different organization. You're not putting away guilt. You're learning to manage the weight of what you've carried."

Aurora settled into position, focusing on her breathing as Raven had taught her. The nervous energy was there, but it felt like anticipation rather than dread. She could do this. She had the skills now.

"Close your eyes," Raven guided softly. "Let the memory come."

The memory unfolded with startling clarity. Aurora was at Bellwater Clearing, having come to check on some plants or perhaps just seeking solitude. The day had been peaceful until she saw Tobias in the pond. At first, she thought he was just swimming. Nothing unusual for someone who controlled water magic.

Tobias emerged from the water, his movements deliberate and desperate. He can breathe underwater, Aurora remembered thinking. Why would he come up for air?

And then she saw him gather his magic, saw the massive boulder at the edge of the clearing lift into the air with terrifying purpose. In that split second, she understood what was happening, and her earth magic responded before her conscious mind could even form the command.

The boulder shattered mid-flight, stone exploding in a shower of fragments that rained harmlessly into the water. The sound was deafening, rock meeting magic in a violent collision that echoed across the clearing like thunder.

Tobias collapsed immediately, the fight going out of him as completely as if someone had cut his strings. Aurora was already running, crashing through the water to reach him, pulling him onto the shore as he broke down completely.

"I have nothing left, Aurora," he sobbed into her shoulder, his whole body shaking. "Hunter left. He just... left. I have no one."

The memory continued to unfold—Aurora's desperate attempts to comfort him, the hours-long conversation by the pond where she used every skill she possessed to rebuild his will to live. She made promises about the future, about things getting better, about how much he mattered to people who loved him.

"I couldn't let his parents down," Aurora whispered, still deep in the memory. "I couldn't let him down."

She felt again the relief when Tobias finally agreed to come home with her, mixed with a terror that felt fresh even now. What if this happened again? What if next time she was too late?

"That was when I started watching him constantly," Aurora realized, her voice thick with understanding. "When I became afraid to let him out of my sight."

"Stay with the memory," Raven instructed gently. "Feel the weight of it, but don't let it overwhelm you. You're organizing now, not drowning."

Aurora began to separate the different threads of the experience—the fear, the success, the crushing responsibility, the love. The memory felt enormous, too important to file away, but Raven's voice guided her through the process.

"You're not filing away the success," Raven reminded her. "You're organizing the overwhelm. The fact that you saved him doesn't go away. But the crushing weight of 'what if' can be managed."

Working carefully, Aurora created multiple organizational spaces in her mind. "Times I Protected Tobias Successfully," "Understanding His Depression," "My Fears About Losing Him." She learned to hold the positive aspects of the memory while organizing the traumatic elements that had been poisoning everything else.

When the breakthrough came, it was like suddenly being able to breathe after holding her breath for years. "I can remember saving him," Aurora said in wonder, "without drowning in the fear of losing him."

She opened her eyes to find Raven watching her with satisfaction. "How do you feel?"

"Different," Aurora said slowly, testing the edges of the organized memory. "I can see how this memory informed everything that came after. This is when I started trying to control everything around him."

They moved outside, both women needing the fresh air to process what had been accomplished. Aurora felt the understanding settle into place like pieces of a puzzle finally fitting together.

AURORA

"I was so terrified of failing him again that I stopped letting him make his own choices," she said, her voice carrying a mixture of grief and clarity. "I saved his life, but then I started suffocating it."

Raven nodded knowingly. "I did the same thing with my son after I saved him. We think if we just control enough variables, we can prevent all pain. But protection and control are different things."

"I can keep my promise without making all his decisions for him," Aurora said, feeling the truth of it resonate through her newly organized understanding. "I can be his protector without being his captor."

As the day progressed, Aurora practiced the technique on smaller memories—times she'd helped other students, moments of effective leadership where the weight of responsibility had felt overwhelming. Each successful organization built her confidence and skill.

By evening, she was able to review the boulder memory again without being crushed by it. She could access the love and success while managing the terror and responsibility that had once made the memory feel impossible to bear.

"If I can organize the day I saved his life," Aurora said as she settled into sleep, "maybe I can handle the day I failed him."

Raven smiled from across the shelter. "One memory at a time, Aurora. You're building exactly the skills you need."

Aurora closed her eyes, practicing the day's technique on the smaller emotional experiences of the day itself. Her magic remained stable throughout, and she could sense the continued healthy growth of plants around the shelter.

She was healing. Not quickly, not painlessly, but thoroughly. And tomorrow, she would be ready to tackle something even more challenging.

"One memory at a time," she whispered to herself, "I'll become who I need to be."

CHAPTER ELEVEN:
The Investigation

Tobias sat hunched over his desk in the principal's office, surrounded by stacks of financial documents that seemed to multiply with each passing hour. The morning light filtering through the dusty windows only emphasized the gravity of what lay before him: month after month of bank statements showing a steady, devastating decline.

He picked up another envelope, this one marked "FINAL NOTICE" in angry red letters. The electricity bill. Due in three days, with a balance that made his stomach churn. Next to it sat the mortgage statement for the main safe house—the one that housed Foxton, Finnian, and the other students. Past due by two months.

"How did Aurora manage all this?" he muttered, running his hands through his already disheveled hair.

The answer became clearer as he dug deeper into the correspondence files. Letter after letter from magical families who had been longtime supporters of Bellwater—donors whose monthly contributions had kept the lights on and the students fed. But the letters grew increasingly frustrated as the months progressed.

AURORA

"Ms. Wildwood, we wrote to you three months ago requesting a progress report on our sponsored student. We've received no response..."

"Aurora, this is the fifth letter we've sent asking about the status of our annual donation. Please confirm receipt..."

"To Whom It May Concern: Without proper communication regarding our financial contributions, we must suspend all future donations until we receive adequate reporting..."

Tobias felt sick. Aurora had simply... ignored them all. Every letter, every concerned email, every phone call had gone unanswered. And now the consequences were catching up to them like a tidal wave.

He pulled up the bank statements on his computer, cross-referencing them with the donation records Aurora had kept. The pattern was devastating: donations that had once flowed in regularly—five thousand here, ten thousand there, sometimes as much as twenty thousand from the wealthier magical families—had dwindled to nothing over the past six months.

The genius of Aurora's system became apparent as he studied the financial flow. She would deposit the magical community's donations into Bellwater Academy's legitimate bank account, then use her authority as guidance counselor, and eventual interim principal, to pay the bills for their safe houses and operations. To Percival Ion, it had looked like standard school expenses; housing assistance for homeless students, tutoring programs, after-school activities. The large homeless population in Bellwater had provided perfect cover for the unconventional expenses.

But without Aurora's reputation and relationships, without her carefully maintained network of donors, the entire funding structure was collapsing like a house of cards.

Tobias's phone buzzed with a text from the property management company: "Final notice: Safe house #3 scheduled for foreclosure proceedings next week unless full payment received."

His heart sank. That was where some of their newer students lived. Where would they go? What would happen to them?

The harsh ring of the school's main phone line jolted him from his spiraling thoughts. Through the office window, he could see Beatrice answering with her usual efficiency, though her expression grew increasingly grim as the conversation progressed.

She knocked on his door moments later.

"Tobias," she said, her voice carrying an edge he never heard before. "Dr. Harrington is here. With a full investigation team from the state."

The blood drained from Tobias's face. "A full team?"

"Education specialists, financial auditors, child welfare investigators." Beatrice's eyes seemed to gleam with something that might have been satisfaction. "They'll be conducting comprehensive interviews with all staff and students."

Tobias wanted to ask her if she had something to do with this, wanted to demand answers about her sudden change in attitude since Percival's death. But he couldn't. Not in front of whatever state officials might be listening.

"Send them in," he managed.

Dr. Harrington entered first, followed by a parade of official-looking individuals carrying clipboards, laptops, and briefcases. The small office suddenly felt claustrophobic.

"Mr. Thornfield," Dr. Harrington said, her tone considerably colder than their previous encounter. "I'm afraid this visit is somewhat more... formal than our last meeting."

"I see that," Tobias replied, trying to keep his voice steady.

"We've received multiple reports raising serious concerns about this institution. Financial irregularities, staffing inconsistencies, and," she paused, consulting her notes, "some rather unusual physical evidence found on the premises."

Tobias's blood turned to ice. "Physical evidence?"

"We'll get to that. First, we need to conduct thorough interviews with your staff and students. I trust you'll provide full cooperation?"

It wasn't really a question.

The next several hours passed in a blur of barely contained panic. Tobias watched helplessly as his carefully constructed world began to unravel, one interview at a time.

From his office, he could hear fragments of conversations as staff members were questioned in the conference room down the hall. Agatha's voice carried the loudest, her disdain for authority figures on full display.

"Family emergency?" one investigator was asking. "And you said Ms. Braithwaite, Mr. Rodson, and Ms. Wildwood all left on the same day?"

"That's right," Agatha replied cheerfully. "Terrible shame, really. Though I suppose when life calls, you answer. Unless you're dead, of course. Then you can't answer anything. Rather difficult to talk when you're six feet under, wouldn't you say?"

Tobias cringed. Agatha's dark humor was not helping their cause.

"Ma'am, are you making light of this situation?" The investigator sounded increasingly irritated.

"Oh, heavens no! I would never make light of the dead. They're quite serious company, the dead. No sense of humor whatsoever."

The questioning grew more intense after that, Tobias noted with growing dread. Agatha's flippant attitude was doing them no favors.

When they brought in Matilda, her responses were maddeningly casual. Tobias strained to hear as she answered questions about the rapid staff turnover with an almost bored indifference.

"People come and go," he heard her say with a shrug he could practically hear in her voice. "It's the nature of education these days. Very competitive field. Everyone's always looking for better opportunities."

"Three teachers and a guidance counselor all left within two weeks," the investigator pressed. "That seems unusual."

"Does it? I suppose you'd know better than I would. I don't really keep track of these things. Not my department."

Tobias buried his head in his hands. Matilda's nonchalant attitude was somehow worse than Agatha's hostile humor.

The student interviews were equally disastrous. Despite their careful preparation, both Foxton and Finnian managed to raise red flags.

"Private lessons with Mr. T?" he heard an investigator ask Foxton. "What kind of private lessons?"

"Oh, just... extra help. You know, tutoring and stuff." Foxton's voice carried a nervous energy that made Tobias's stomach twist.

"Tutoring in what subjects?"

"Uh... life skills? Study habits?" The uncertainty in Foxton's voice was painful to hear.

When they questioned Finnian, his analytical nature worked against them.

"The tutoring sessions," Finnian explained with his characteristic precision, "follow a very specific curriculum structure that emphasizes practical application of theoretical concepts through controlled environmental exercises."

Tobias could practically hear the investigators' eyebrows raising. Finnian was making their "tutoring" sound far more sophisticated and secretive than any normal high school program.

"And these sessions take place...?"

AURORA

"At various off-site locations, depending on the specific learning objectives for each session."

Tobias wanted to scream. They might as well have hung a billboard that read "SECRET MAGIC TRAINING" over the school entrance.

The worst came when he overheard fragments of parent interviews. Local families; the "normal", non-magical ones whose children attended Bellwater Academy, were expressing serious concerns.

"We're worried about the stability," one mother was saying. "Our daughter mentioned that several of her favorite teachers just… disappeared. And now a teacher who was fired is suddenly the principal? It doesn't inspire confidence."

"The school seems different," another parent added. "There are all these new students living in what they call 'safe houses,' but nobody explains where they came from or why they need housing. And my son says they have special classes that other students aren't allowed to attend."

Each comment was another nail in their coffin. Tobias could see how it all looked to outside observers: a school in chaos, with unexplained changes, secret programs, and a leadership transition that raised more questions than it answered.

But the death blow came when Dr. Harrington emerged from the basement, her face pale and her eyes wide with something between confusion and alarm.

"Mr. Thornfield," she said, her voice tight with barely controlled shock. "I need you to explain what we found downstairs."

Tobias's heart stopped. The basement. Where Aurora had tortured Marina. Where the final confrontation with Sabrina and Lucien had taken place. He'd been so focused on the financial crisis and staffing issues that he completely forgot about the physical evidence that might remain.

"I'm not sure what you mean," he said weakly.

Dr. Harrington gestured to one of the investigators, who opened a tablet and showed Tobias a series of photographs. Scorch marks covered the walls in patterns that defied explanation. Deep gouges on the concrete floor looked like something had been dragged across it with tremendous force. Dark stains that could only be blood dotted the surfaces. Most damning of all were the metal chains still bolted to the wall. Chains that no normal basement would ever need.

"Mr. Thornfield," Dr. Harrington said slowly, "this looks like a torture chamber."

The room spun around Tobias. How could he possibly explain this? That his predecessor had held an enemy combatant here? That magical battles had been fought in this space? That the blood and burn marks were the result of elemental magic clashing in desperate combat?

"I... I honestly don't know," he stammered. "I've only been principal for a few weeks. I wasn't aware of... whatever this is."

The investigator's expression made it clear she didn't believe a word of it.

As the day wore on, Tobias felt the walls closing in. Every answer led to more questions. Every explanation raised new suspicions. The magical evidence was too obvious, the timing too convenient, the cover stories too thin.

He found himself wondering obsessively about who could have called in the investigation. Beatrice seemed the most likely suspect; her loyalty to Percival Ion had been absolute, and she'd never hidden her disdain for the way things had changed since his death. But what about Sabrina and Lucien? They vanished right before this all started. Had they somehow orchestrated this as a final blow against Aurora's legacy?

The paranoia ate at him as he watched his carefully constructed world crumble. He failed. Failed to protect the school, failed to protect the students, failed to maintain the delicate balance that had kept their magical community hidden and safe.

Dr. Harrington called the final meeting as the afternoon light began to fade. All remaining staff and students were gathered in the main hallway, their faces reflecting the same mixture of confusion and fear that Tobias felt in his bones.

"After careful consideration of all evidence gathered during today's investigation," Dr. Harrington announced, her voice carrying the weight of finality, "I am hereby ordering the closure of Bellwater Academy, effective immediately."

The words hit like physical blows. Students gasped. Agatha swore colorfully. Foxton and Finnian exchanged looks of barely concealed panic.

"All students have forty-eight hours to make alternative educational arrangements," Dr. Harrington continued. "School accounts are frozen, pending comprehensive audit. All staff are dismissed, and the building is sealed until further notice."

Tobias watched the faces around him; his students, his colleagues, the young people he swore to protect. The weight of total failure settled on his shoulders like a lead blanket.

As the investigators packed up their equipment and the small crowd began to disperse, Tobias found himself alone in the empty hallway. The fluorescent lights hummed overhead, casting harsh shadows on walls that had witnessed so much—both wonderful and terrible.

Foxton approached hesitantly, Finnian close behind.

"Mr. T," Foxton said quietly, "what happens now?"

Tobias looked at their faces—so young, so trusting, so frightened—and realized he had no answer. The safe houses were in foreclosure. The school was closed. Their funding was gone. Their cover was blown.

"I don't know," he admitted, the words tasting like ash in his mouth. "I honestly don't know."

CHAPTER TWELVE:
Consequences

Tobias sat in Aurora's cottage, staring at his phone. The silence was deafening after the chaos of the day. Forty-eight hours. That's how long his students had to figure out their lives before they were officially homeless. The cottage felt different now, not like the warm refuge it had once been, but like a museum of better times.

He drove to the cottage on autopilot after watching the last of the investigators leave, after seeing the fear in Foxton and Finnian's eyes, after locking the doors to Bellwater Academy for what might be the final time. The financial documents were still spread across Aurora's kitchen table where he'd left them that morning, each one a testament to how thoroughly everything had fallen apart.

His phone sat heavy in his hands. Three months. Hunter and Odion had been searching for Aurora for three months while Tobias held everything together. While he managed the school, dealt with parents, trained students, and somehow kept their entire world from collapsing. They had to have something by now. Some lead, some progress, some hope.

With mechanical precision, he opened his contacts and started a group FaceTime call.

The screen split as both Hunter and Odion answered almost simultaneously. They looked tired, sitting in what appeared to be a hotel room.

"Toby!" Odion said, his face brightening. "How are things going? We weren't expecting—"

"Progress report," Tobias interrupted, his voice eerily calm. "I need to know where we stand with the search."

Hunter and Odion exchanged a glance across the screen.

"Well," Hunter began slowly, "we've been following several leads—"

"Specifics," Tobias said, settling back in his chair like this was just another teacher's union meeting. "What concrete progress have you made? What's our timeline? What resources do you need?"

The silence stretched uncomfortably long.

"Toby," Odion said gently, "maybe we should talk about how you're doing first. You sound—"

"I'm fine. Aurora's been missing for three months. The Bellwater Mages need their leader back. What have you found?"

Another pause. Then Hunter cleared his throat. "We've identified several possible locations where she might be hiding. We're working through them systematically—"

"Working through them how? What's your methodology? How many locations? How are you prioritizing them?"

"Jesus, Toby," Hunter muttered. "It's not a military operation—"

"It should be." Tobias's voice remained flat, professional. "We have students to protect, a school to run, a community to maintain. Aurora has responsibilities. Where is she?"

Movement on Odion's side of the screen caught his attention. Someone was walking into the frame—a young woman with long blue hair.

Tobias looked at her, recognizing her. Then he realized where he had seen her.

The sight of her hit Tobias like a physical blow. Suddenly he was back in the basement, watching Aurora strangle her with thorny vines, listening to her screams, cleaning up the blood afterward. The careful compartmentalization he maintained all day cracked.

"What is she doing there?" His voice was no longer calm, but panicked.

Odion glanced over at Marina, then back at the camera. "Oh, Marina's been helping us with—"

"Helping you? With what, exactly?" The words came out sharper than intended.

"With the search," Hunter interjected. "She knows the Rebellion's old hideouts better than anyone—"

"The search." Tobias repeated the words slowly, like he was tasting something bitter. "Right. The search that's produced no results in three months."

"Toby, that's not fair—" Odion started.

"Isn't it?" Something was building in Tobias's chest, hot and tight. "Three months, Odion. Three months while I've been holding everything together. While I've been dealing with state investigations and financial audits and students who have nowhere to live. Three months while our entire world has been falling apart."

"We didn't know things were that bad," Hunter said, his brow furrowing with concern.

"Of course you didn't know!" Tobias's voice finally cracked, the careful control shattering. "Because you've been too busy playing house with your new girlfriend to actually focus on finding Aurora!"

Odion's face went white. "What are you talking about?"

"Don't." Tobias stood up abruptly, the phone shaking in his hands.

"Don't you dare pretend this is about the search. I saw you two together at the warehouse, Odion. I saw how you looked at her. And now here she is, conveniently staying with you while Aurora is God knows where and our entire operation is collapsing!"

"Toby, you're not thinking clearly—"

"I'm thinking perfectly clearly!" Tobias was yelling now, months of suppressed panic and exhaustion pouring out. "I'm thinking that while I've been drowning trying to keep everything afloat, you two have been playing at being investigators so you could justify your little romance!"

Marina stepped fully into view, her face pale but determined. "That's not what's happening here. We've been working every day to—"

"Working on what? Your relationship?" Tobias's laugh was bitter, borderline hysterical. "The school is closed, Odion! Closed! The state seized all our assets. Our students are going to be homeless in forty-eight hours. And you're shacked up with the girl who got us into this mess in the first place!"

"That's enough!" Hunter's voice cut through the tirade. "Toby, you need to calm down and listen—"

"Listen to what? More excuses? More lies?" Tobias was pacing now, the phone's camera catching wild glimpses of Aurora's cottage. "I've been waiting for you to bring her home, and instead you've been—"

"We've been searching!" Odion shouted back, his own composure finally cracking. "But it's kind of hard to know where she went, Tobias! It's not like she left us a map!"

"And what do you have to show for your 'search'? Where is she?"

The silence that followed was deafening. Hunter and Odion stared at him through the screen, both looking stricken.

"We don't know," Hunter admitted quietly.

The words hit Tobias like a slap. All the fight went out of him at once, leaving him hollow and exhausted.

"Then we've lost," he whispered, sinking back into the chair. "We've lost everything."

"No, we haven't." Marina's voice cut through the despair, clear and steady. "We've lost time, and we've lost ground, but we haven't lost everything."

Tobias looked at her through the screen, really looked at her for the first time since she appeared. Not as a symbol of Aurora's failures or evidence of Odion's supposed distraction, but as a person who had been working to solve this too.

"The school's gone," he said flatly. "The funding's gone. The students—"

"Are still alive," Marina interrupted. "And so are we. And Aurora is still out there somewhere."

"You don't understand," Tobias began, but Hunter spoke over him.

"No, you don't understand." Hunter's face was grim but determined. "We haven't been sitting around doing nothing, Toby. We've narrowed it down. We know she's not in any of the major cities. We know she's avoiding all the old Rebellion strongholds. We know—"

"We know she's somewhere rural," Odion added, his anger from moments before replaced by urgency. "Somewhere she can lay low. And Marina's been tracking financial patterns that—"

"Shut up," Tobias said quietly. They all stopped talking. "Just... shut up for a second." He rubbed his temples, trying to think through the exhaustion. "How much money do you have left?"

The question seemed to catch them off guard. "What?" Odion asked.

"Money. Cash. Credit limits. How much?"

Hunter and Odion exchanged glances. "Maybe three hundred between us?" Hunter said. "We've been staying in cheap places, but—"

"The rental car?"

"Due back tomorrow," Odion confirmed.

Tobias nodded slowly. "Return it today. Check out of the hotel. We can't afford to keep burning money on this search."

"Toby, we need transportation—"

"You can teleport." Tobias was thinking out loud now, the practical side of his brain finally kicking in. "Both of you. How far are you from here?"

"About six hundred miles," Hunter answered cautiously.

"That's doable," Tobias said. "Difficult, but doable. Especially if you do it in stages."

"You want us to come back?"

"I want us to be in the same place so we can actually coordinate this search instead of fumbling around separately." Tobias's voice was steadier now, more focused. "We need to pool our resources, share what we know, and figure out a real plan."

"What about the students?" Odion asked. "Foxton and Finnian and the others?"

"They'll have to manage for forty-eight hours. Maybe longer." The words tasted bitter, but Tobias forced them out. "If we don't find Aurora, it won't matter where they go to school."

Marina leaned closer to the camera. "There's something else. Something we found but haven't had a chance to verify."

"What?"

"A pattern in the magical disturbances," she said. "Small things, barely noticeable unless you know what to look for. But there's been activity in three specific regions over the past month."

Tobias felt something like hope stirring in his chest. "Where?"

"That's what we need to figure out together," Hunter said. "We have the data, but we need someone who knows Aurora better than we do to help interpret it."

"Someone who understands how she thinks," Odion added, looking directly at Tobias.

For the first time in hours, Tobias felt like he could breathe. "How long will it take you to get here?"

"If we leave now and do it in two or three jumps?" Hunter calculated quickly. "Six hours, maybe seven. We should rest between jumps. Teleportation takes a lot out of you at the best of times, as you know."

"Do it." Tobias was already thinking ahead, mentally cataloging what resources they had left at the cottage, what information he could gather while he waited. "And bring everything. Every scrap of information, every lead, every theory. We're going to find her."

The connection ended, leaving Tobias alone in the cottage again. But this time, the silence felt different. Not empty, but expectant. Like the pause before something important began.

He looked at his watch. Six hours, maybe seven. That gave him time to do one thing he should have done hours ago.

The drive to the safe house took fifteen minutes through the quiet streets of Bellwater. The house looked smaller somehow in the fading daylight, less like a refuge and more like what it really was: a temporary shelter for displaced kids who had nowhere else to go.

Tobias knocked on the door, hearing voices fall silent inside. Foxton answered, his face brightening with relief.

"Mr. T! We didn't know if you were coming back."

"Of course I'm coming back." Tobias stepped inside, finding Finnian sitting at the kitchen table with what looked like homework spread out in front of him. "How are you two holding up?"

"Okay, I guess," Foxton said, though his voice carried an uncertainty that made Tobias's chest tighten. "Finnian's been researching alternative schools online. You know, just in case."

Finnian looked up from his laptop. "There are several options within commuting distance. Not ideal, but manageable if we can maintain housing here."

The practicality in Finnian's voice—the assumption that they'd need backup plans, that Bellwater Academy was really gone—hit Tobias harder than he expected.

"I'm sorry," he said quietly, sinking into one of the kitchen chairs. "I'm sorry that Sabrina and Lucien, or maybe Beatrice, had to ruin this for you. Someone called in that investigation, and—"

"Mr. T," Foxton interrupted gently. "What if it wasn't them?"

Tobias frowned. "What do you mean?"

Finnian closed his laptop, his analytical mind clearly already working through the problem. "We've been talking about it all afternoon. The timeline, the evidence they found, the questions they were asking."

"And?"

"The basement," Foxton said simply. "They found the basement where Aurora..." He trailed off, not wanting to say the words.

"Where she tortured Marina," Finnian finished clinically. "That's what triggered this, isn't it? Someone saw something, or heard something, or Aurora left too much evidence behind."

Tobias felt something cold settle in his stomach. "You think Aurora caused this investigation?"

"Not intentionally," Finnian said quickly. "But think about it logically. The massacre of police officers made the news. A guidance counselor suddenly becoming principal after the previous principal died mysteriously. Financial irregularities that Aurora created with her funding system. Staff disappearing without explanation. And then physical evidence of torture in the school basement."

Foxton sat down across from Tobias, his expression more serious than his eighteen years should have required. "Mr. T, what if this isn't about enemies trying to destroy us? What if it's just... consequences?"

The word hung in the air like an accusation. Consequences. Not sabotage, not betrayal, not external enemies, just the natural result of Aurora's increasingly destructive choices finally catching up with them.

"She was trying to protect us," Tobias said weakly.

"Was she?" Finnian asked, not unkindly. "Or was she protecting herself? Her position, her authority, her way of doing things?"

Tobias stared at the table, his mind racing through the last few months. Aurora strangling Elena with a sunflower for a disrespectful comment. Torturing Marina in the basement. Massacring police officers rather than finding another way out. Ignoring donor correspondence until their funding collapsed. Each decision escalating the danger, creating new problems instead of solving existing ones.

"I need to go," he said abruptly, standing up.

"Mr. T—" Foxton started.

"I'll figure this out," Tobias promised, though he wasn't sure what 'this' even was anymore. "Just... give me a little more time."

He left them sitting in the kitchen, two teenagers who'd lost everything but somehow saw the situation more clearly than he did. As he drove back to the cottage, Foxton's words echoed in his mind: *What if it's just consequences?*

CHAPTER THIRTEEN:
Questions Without Answers

For the first time since arriving at Raven's shelter, Aurora felt genuinely optimistic about the future. The memory work was progressing faster than she'd dared hope, and each successful organization brought her closer to the person she needed to be.

She sat up, testing her magical stability as had become her morning routine. The earth beneath her felt solid and responsive rather than chaotic. Around the shelter, plants showed healthy growth—small flowers pushing through soil that had been barren just days before. Her magic was healing along with her mind.

"When I go back to Bellwater," she said aloud, practicing the words, "I'll be able to handle conflicts without losing control. I'll be the protector Tobias needs me to be."

The words felt good to say. Hopeful. Like a promise she could actually keep this time.

"Good morning," Raven said when Aurora entered the shelter, her voice carrying that familiar note of cautious observation. "You seem... confident today."

"I feel confident," Aurora replied, settling into their usual morning routine. "Yesterday's work with the boulder memory was a breakthrough. I can finally separate my success from my fear, my protection from my control." She accepted the cup of herbal tea Raven offered. "When I go back to Bellwater, I'll be able to support Tobias properly instead of suffocating him."

Raven's expression remained neutral, but Aurora caught a flicker of something—concern, perhaps?—in the older woman's eyes. "You've made excellent progress," Raven agreed carefully. "Are you ready to work with another significant memory today?"

"Absolutely." Aurora's confidence was unshakeable. "I want to tackle one of the bigger ones. Something that really shaped how I've been relating to Tobias."

"Tell me about a time when you thought you were protecting him, but things didn't go the way you expected."

Aurora didn't hesitate. The memory came to mind immediately, one she'd thought about often over the years as evidence of her necessary vigilance.

"The Hunter situation," she said. "When I realized Hunter was becoming too possessive, too dependent on Tobias in an unhealthy way. I had to intervene before it destroyed them both."

Raven arranged some stones in the now-familiar pattern. She had used these stones a few times before; she called them her "memory stones" and refused to say more on the subject. "Tell me more about that."

"It was maybe five years ago," Aurora began, settling into the cross-legged position that had become second nature. "Hunter and Tobias were... very close. Best friends, but Hunter wanted more. I could see it in the way he looked at Tobias, the way he monopolized his time. Tobias was so trusting, so willing to believe the best in people, that he couldn't see how unhealthy the dynamic was becoming."

She closed her eyes, letting the memory take shape. "Hunter was suffocating him, making all these demands on his time and emotional energy. Toby was getting thin, exhausted, because he felt responsible for Hunter's happiness. I knew I had to do something."

"What did you do?"

"I had a talk with Hunter. Made it clear that his behavior was inappropriate, that he needed to give Tobias space to breathe. When that didn't work, I... intervened more directly."

The memory unfolded with crystal clarity now. Aurora was back at Bellwater Clearing, confronting Hunter after she'd witnessed yet another instance of his possessive behavior.

"You need to back off," she'd told him bluntly. "Tobias is not your property."

"I don't know what you're talking about," Hunter had replied, but his defensive posture told a different story.

"I'm talking about the way you monopolize his time. The way you get jealous when he spends time with anyone else. The way you make your emotional state his responsibility." Aurora had felt so righteous in that moment, so certain she was protecting Tobias from harm.

But as she continued through the memory, guided by Raven's gentle prompts to examine every detail, something uncomfortable began to emerge.

"Stay with that feeling of certainty," Raven instructed. "What was driving it?"

Aurora focused on her younger self, analyzing her motivations with the clarity her memory work had taught her. "I was... I was terrified," she realized slowly. "Terrified that Hunter would hurt Tobias, that he'd break his heart or damage his trust in people."

"And?"

There was something else, something deeper. Aurora probed carefully, like touching a bruise to see how much it hurt. "I was afraid Hunter would replace me," she whispered.

The admission hit her like a physical blow. In the memory, she could see now--the way her righteousness had been colored by possessiveness, the way her concern for Tobias had been mixed with fear of losing her central place in his life.

"I told myself I was protecting him," Aurora said, her voice thick with realization. "But I was also protecting my position as his primary support system."

The memory continued to unfold, but now Aurora could see the layers she'd missed before. How she'd presented the situation to Tobias in ways that emphasized Hunter's flaws while downplaying his genuine care. How she'd gradually isolated Tobias from Hunter under the guise of protection.

"I didn't just intervene," she said quietly. "I manipulated the situation to drive them apart."

"Why?" Raven's voice was gentle but relentless.

Aurora sat with the question, feeling the weight of it. "Because... because if Tobias didn't need me anymore, what would I be?"

The truth of it was devastating. All her protective instincts, all her fierce loyalty—how much of it had been genuine love, and how much had been fear of irrelevance?

"Tobias did need space from Hunter," she said defensively. "Hunter was being possessive and unhealthy—"

"That may be true," Raven agreed. "But examine your methods. What would protecting Tobias look like if you didn't need anything in return?"

The question hit Aurora like a truck. If she didn't need to be needed, if she didn't require gratitude or central importance in his life, how would

AURORA

she have handled the Hunter situation differently?

"I would have... talked to Tobias directly," she said slowly. "Asked him how he felt about the relationship. Helped him set his own boundaries instead of setting them for him."

"And if he'd chosen to maintain his friendship with Hunter despite the problems?"

Aurora felt something twist in her chest. "I would have... supported his choice. Been there if things went wrong, but let him make his own mistakes."

"Instead?"

"Instead, I made the choice for him. Took away his agency under the pretense of protection." Aurora opened her eyes, meeting Raven's steady gaze. "I was so afraid of losing him that I made sure no one else could have him either."

They worked in silence for a while, Aurora carefully organizing the different threads of the memory. The genuine concern for Tobias's wellbeing went into one mental file. The fear and possessiveness went into another. The recognition of her manipulation into a third.

When she was finished, Aurora felt hollow but clear. The memory was still there, but it no longer felt like a triumph of protective love. It felt like what it was: a moment when her fear had overridden her wisdom, when her need had disguised itself as care.

"How do you feel?" Raven asked.

"Ashamed," Aurora said honestly. "But also... confused. If I can't trust my own protective instincts, how do I know when I'm genuinely helping versus when I'm just feeding my own needs?"

"What would loving Tobias without needing anything in return look like?"

"I don't know," she whispered.

"If you truly put his wellbeing first, what would that require?"

Aurora stared at the ground, her mind racing. "It would require... letting him make his own choices. Even bad ones. It would require supporting his decisions even when I disagreed with them. It would require..." She paused, the words catching in her throat. "It would require accepting that he might not need me."

"And how does that possibility feel?"

"Terrifying," Aurora admitted. "If Tobias doesn't need me, then who am I? What's my purpose?"

Raven nodded knowingly. "Those are the questions that lead to real healing, Aurora. Not 'How can I become worthy of being needed again?' but 'Who am I when I'm not needed?'"

They spent the rest of the morning working through smaller memories, each one revealing similar patterns. Moments when Aurora had convinced herself she was protecting Tobias while actually protecting her own position in his life. Times when she'd made his problems about her failure rather than about his needs.

By afternoon, Aurora felt exhausted but oddly clear. As she practiced her memory organization techniques, a stray thought flickered through her mind: *What if Tobias is happier without me?*

The thought was there and gone in an instant, too frightening to fully examine. She pushed it away, focusing instead on the work at hand. But it left a strange taste in her mouth, like the aftertaste of something bitter.

"Raven," she said as they prepared their evening meal, "how did you know that staying away from your son was the right choice?"

Raven paused in her stirring, considering the question carefully. "Because when I imagined him with me versus him without me, the version without me was healthier. Safer. Happier."

AURORA

"But didn't that hurt? Knowing he was better off without you?"

"It nearly killed me," Raven said simply. "But love isn't about what makes us feel good, Aurora. It's about what serves the beloved."

Aurora nodded, filing the comment away for later examination. As they settled into their evening routine, she found herself speaking more tentatively than she had that morning.

"When I'm ready to see Tobias again," she said, then paused. "If I'm ready. If that's what's best for him."

Raven smiled sadly. "Now you're asking the right questions."

Aurora lay awake that night, staring at the ceiling of the mountain shelter. For months, she'd been focused on becoming worthy of returning to Tobias, of reclaiming her place in his life. But Raven's questions had opened up possibilities she'd never considered.

What if the most loving thing she could do was stay away? What if her return would simply restart old patterns of control and manipulation? What if Tobias was better, stronger, healthier without her constant interference?

The thoughts were too painful to fully examine, but they lingered at the edges of her consciousness like shadows. For the first time since beginning her healing work, Aurora fell asleep without planning for her eventual return.

Instead, she dreamed of Tobias laughing with friends she didn't know, making choices she hadn't influenced, living a life that was entirely his own.

In the dream, he looked happier than she'd ever seen him.

CHAPTER FOURTEEN:
The Mirror of Control

"Good morning," Raven said when Aurora entered the main room, her voice carrying that familiar note of cautious observation. She studied Aurora's face carefully. "You've been making remarkable progress with the difficult memories. Perhaps today we should examine one of your successes, a time when your intervention truly helped Tobias."

Aurora's eyes lit up immediately. "Yes! I'd love to work with something positive for once. I want to understand what healthy protection actually looks like so I can replicate it when I return."

"Tell me about a moment when you guided Tobias well."

Aurora settled into position without hesitation. "When I convinced him to substitute teach for Agatha last October. It was exactly what he needed—a chance to connect with students again, to remember why he loved teaching. He was resistant at first, but I helped him see the opportunity."

Raven arranged her stones with deliberate care. "Show me how that unfolded."

"It was brilliant," Aurora said, closing her eyes. "The students responded to him immediately. He found his confidence again, remembered his passion for education. I knew it would be perfect for him."

The memory crystallized around Aurora like stepping into a photograph. She was back in her cluttered office at Bellwater Academy, emergency papers scattered everywhere. Agatha's broken hip had left them desperately short-staffed, and the students couldn't be left with just anyone.

"These kids need you, Tobias," past-Aurora was saying, her voice urgent with conviction. "After everything they've been through, they deserve someone who actually understands trauma, someone who sees them as whole people instead of problems to manage."

Tobias sat across from her, shoulders tense with visible reluctance. "Aurora, I appreciate the vote of confidence, but this feels like a mistake. Percival already thinks I'm a troublemaker. Putting me in front of his students seems like asking for disaster."

"You're not thinking about this clearly," Aurora pressed, leaning forward with the intensity that had always served her well in crisis situations. "These students have already lost so much. They need consistency, not whoever the district sends as a warm body."

"But what if I mess this up?" Tobias's voice carried that familiar thread of self-doubt that always made Aurora want to wrap him in reassurance. "What if I say something wrong and make everything worse for everyone?"

Aurora felt her younger self's impatience flare—the righteous frustration of someone who could see the obvious solution. "So, you're going to abandon these kids because you're scared of Percival's opinion?"

"That's not—" Tobias started, but Aurora was already moving to her next argument.

"Look, I'm telling you this is necessary," she said, her voice taking on the authoritative edge that usually ended discussions. "These students trust me to advocate for them, and I'm advocating for you to be their teacher."

Tobias's expression wavered, caught between his instincts and her certainty. "Aurora, I really think this could backfire—"

"You're catastrophizing again," she interrupted, reaching across to grab his hands. "I need you to trust me on this. You're the only person I can count on to do right by these kids, and they need you whether you can see it or not."

The emotional appeal hit its mark. Tobias's resistance crumbled under the weight of duty and Aurora's unwavering faith in her own judgment. "Okay," he said quietly, though worry lines remained etched around his eyes. "If you really think it's the right thing..."

"I know it is," Aurora assured him with complete confidence. "You'll see. This is going to be exactly what you need."

"Stay with that certainty," Raven's voice brought Aurora back to the present. "What was powering it?"

Aurora smiled, remembering the satisfaction of that moment. "I could see his potential so clearly. Tobias was letting his anxiety make the decision instead of recognizing how much good he could do."

"Walk me through what happened next."

The memory continued its progression. Tobias accepting the position despite his reservations. His initial success with the students, the way they responded to his gentleness and understanding. Aurora's vindication when he seemed to find his rhythm in the classroom.

Then came the crash. Percival's explosion when Tobias shared his political views with impressionable teenagers. The immediate termination. Tobias's devastation as he realized his worst fears had come true.

"He got fired," Aurora said, her voice losing some of its earlier warmth.

"For doing exactly what he was afraid he might do," Raven observed neutrally.

Something cold began spreading through Aurora's chest. "Percival was looking for any excuse to get rid of him—"

"What did Tobias ask you for in that situation?" Raven interrupted gently.

The question felt like stepping on a broken stair. "He... he asked me to trust his judgment about the risks."

"And what did you give him instead?"

Aurora's throat felt suddenly dry. "I gave him my judgment about what was best for the students."

"Were the students your primary concern?"

The memory sharpened with uncomfortable clarity. Aurora could see her past self's motivations now, stripped of the noble justifications she'd wrapped around them. The desperate need to have Tobias more involved in Bellwater operations. The satisfaction of proving she understood his capabilities better than he did. The way his dependence on her guidance had made her feel essential, irreplaceable.

"I wanted him at the school," Aurora whispered. "I wanted him working under my supervision where I could... where I could..."

"Where you could what?"

"Where I could manage his interactions with the world," Aurora finished, the words feeling like poison on her tongue.

"How did you override his resistance?"

Each answer felt like peeling away her own skin. "I questioned his courage. I made it about the students' needs instead of his concerns. I used my authority as guidance counselor...no, as his friend, as his mentor...to pressure him."

"What would respecting his choice have looked like?"

Aurora sat with the devastating simplicity of the question. "I would have found another solution. I would have accepted that he understood the political situation better than I did. I would have..." She paused, the truth almost too painful to voice. "I would have put his wellbeing ahead of my desire to be right."

Raven let the silence stretch before asking, "Tell me about Hunter's approach to Tobias's decisions."

Aurora's mind immediately jumped to Hunter's possessive patterns, his refusal to accept 'no' as an answer. "Hunter would never take Tobias's concerns seriously. He'd just keep pushing different arguments until—"

The parallel hit her like cold water to the face.

"Until Tobias gave in," she completed in a whisper.

The memory stones felt suddenly heavy in her hands. Aurora stared at them, seeing her own reflection fractured across their surfaces. Every criticism she'd ever leveled at Hunter's controlling behavior could be applied to her own actions in that office last October.

"I bullied him into it," she said, her voice hollow with recognition. "I used guilt and authority and emotional manipulation to get my way."

"And justified it how?"

"By telling myself it was for his own good. By convincing myself I knew what he needed better than he did." Aurora's hands began to shake. "Just like Hunter always did."

The room tilted around her as the full scope of her self-deception became clear. She'd spent years condemning Hunter for his possessive refusal to respect Tobias's autonomy, all while employing identical tactics with more sophisticated justifications.

"I'm no different from him," Aurora said, the words coming out strangled. "I just dressed up my control in prettier language."

The careful progress she'd made over the past weeks felt like it was dissolving around her. Every organized memory, every moment of clarity, every piece of growth—it all crumbled under the weight of this recognition. She hadn't been healing; she'd been rearranging her rationalizations.

"The students did need a good teacher," Aurora said desperately, grasping for some thread of justification.

"Yes," Raven agreed. "But was that why you pushed him into it?"

Aurora closed her eyes, forcing herself to examine her true motivations with brutal honesty. "No. I pushed him because I wanted him closer to my world. I wanted to prove I understood his potential better than he understood his own limitations. I wanted…" She took a shuddering breath. "I wanted him to need my guidance."

"And when his concerns proved accurate?"

"I let him blame himself for not being strong enough to handle the politics." The admission felt like swallowing glass. "I let him apologize to me for failing, when really I had failed him by not listening."

Aurora looked around the shelter that had become her sanctuary, seeing now how fragile her supposed progress really was. She'd organized her obvious failures, her moments of violence and loss of control. But she'd left untouched the deeper pattern of manipulation that had defined their entire relationship.

"Every time I 'helped' him make a decision, I was really just wearing him down until he agreed with me," she said, her voice barely audible. "Every time I 'protected' him from making a mistake, I was really protecting myself from watching him choose something I didn't approve of."

The earth beneath the shelter began to respond to her emotional state, small tremors running through the foundation. Aurora felt her magic stirring, feeding off her distress, but she couldn't bring herself to care about containment anymore.

"Don't ever love someone who can't love you back, Aurora," Raven said quietly.

The words landed like a physical blow. Aurora looked up at the older woman, feeling like everything inside her was breaking apart.

"I don't understand."

"The kind of love you've been giving Tobias—the all-consuming, life-defining, identity-shaping devotion—does he feel that same way about you?"

Aurora opened her mouth to say of course he did, then stopped. When had Tobias ever made his life about her the way she'd made hers about him? When had he ever sacrificed his own judgment to preserve their relationship? When had he ever needed her approval to feel confident in his choices?

"I don't know," she whispered.

"And until you do know," Raven said gently, "you'll keep trying to make him love you the way you love him. You'll keep controlling and manipulating and telling yourself it's protection. Because needing someone who doesn't need you back will destroy you both."

CHAPTER FIFTEEN:
The Cost of Distance

The hotel room felt cramped with three people trying to pack quickly. Hunter stuffed his few belongings into a worn duffle bag while Marina folded her clothes with military precision. Odion sat at the small desk with his laptop, furiously calculating distances and magical energy requirements like he was preparing for a final exam.

"Six hundred miles," he muttered, fingers flying across the keyboard. "Two jumps of three hundred each. Totally manageable."

Hunter glanced over at the screen full of numbers and equations. "You sure about this? That's a hell of a lot farther than we've been jumping."

"I can handle it," Odion said, closing the laptop with more force than necessary. "I've been practicing. I know my limits."

Marina looked up from her packing, concern evident in her expression. "Maybe we should consider shorter jumps? Four or five smaller teleportation's instead of two big ones?"

"We don't have time for that," Hunter snapped, zipping his bag closed. "Tobias is expecting us in six hours. He's already dealing with the school closure and God knows what else. The last thing he needs is us taking our sweet time getting there."

Odion stood up, straightening his shoulders. "Marina, I appreciate the concern, but I've done the math. Three hundred miles is within my range, especially with you and Hunter helping to anchor the teleportation."

"It's not about the math," Marina pressed. "It's about the fact that you're not at full strength. None of us are. We've all been through hell in the past few months."

Hunter grabbed his jacket from the back of a chair. "We don't have time to baby anyone. Tobias needs us there, and we're going. Odion says he can do it, so we do it."

Marina opened her mouth to argue further, but Odion held up a hand. "Look, I know you're trying to look out for me, and I get it. But I'm not some fragile newbie anymore. I can handle this."

The determination in his voice was final. She sighed and finished packing her bag.

"Fine. But if you feel even slightly off during the first jump, we stop and reassess. Deal?"

"Deal," Odion agreed, though his tone suggested he thought her concerns were unnecessary.

They checked out of the hotel and walked to an empty field behind the building. The late afternoon sun was beginning to sink toward the horizon, and the air carried the crisp bite of early spring. Hunter looked around to make sure no one was watching, then nodded to Odion.

"You ready for this?"

Odion closed his eyes, centering himself the way Tobias had taught him. "Ready. Everyone hold on."

Hunter and Marina each placed a hand on Odion's shoulders. The familiar sensation of teleportation magic building around them felt different this time—more intense, more demanding. Odion's face was tight with concentration as he visualized their destination three hundred miles away.

The world dissolved around them.

When reality reassembled itself, they were standing in a rural area that looked nothing like the rest stop Odion had been aiming for. Instead of a paved parking lot, they found themselves on the muddy bank of what should have been a river. Instead of rushing water, they stared into an empty crater that stretched out before them like a wound in the earth.

"Where's the water?" Marina whispered, her voice barely audible.

Hunter spun around, looking for Odion, and his heart stopped. The math teacher was collapsed on the ground twenty feet away, his skin pale as winter frost. He wasn't moving.

"ODION!"

Hunter rushed to his side, dropping to his knees beside the unconscious man. Odion's breathing was shallow and rapid, and his skin felt cold to the touch. "Odion, can you hear me?"

Marina appeared beside them, her face grim as she surveyed the empty riverbed. Dead fish lay scattered across the mud, their silver scales dulled and lifeless. The smell of rotting vegetation hung heavy in the air.

"Oh god," she breathed. "He drained it all."

Hunter looked up at her, panic rising in his throat. "What do you mean he drained it all?!"

"This is what happens with severe magical exhaustion," Marina explained, kneeling beside Odion and checking his pulse. "His body used more energy than he had available for the teleportation. Now his magic is pulling energy from everything around him to keep him alive."

As if to prove her point, the grass beneath Odion began to wither and brown. Small wildflowers nearby drooped and crumbled to dust. The very air around him seemed to shimmer with the magical drain.

"We have to do something," Hunter said, his voice tight with fear. "How do we stop it?!"

"I don't know if we can," Marina replied, her hands hovering over Odion's still form. "His magic is in survival mode. It's going to keep draining energy from anything nearby until it stabilizes or..." She trailed off, but the implication was clear.

Hunter felt something he hadn't experienced in years: complete helplessness. "There has to be something. Some way to help him."

Marina was quiet for a moment, her eyes distant as she thought. "Actually," she said slowly, "there might be. It's risky, but I learned something from my grandmother years ago. For magical shock."

"What kind of something?"

"I have to freeze him," Marina said, her voice growing more confident as the plan formed. "Encase him in ice to stop the magical drain long enough for me to prepare a remedy."

Hunter stared at her like she'd suggested setting Odion on fire. "You want to turn him into a popsicle?!"

"Trust me or watch him die," Marina said firmly. "The ice will slow down his magical processes, give us time to help him. But I need you to work with me on this."

Hunter looked down at Odion, whose breathing was becoming more labored by the minute. The grass around him was now completely dead, and the magical drain was spreading outward in an ever-widening circle.

"Do it," he said quietly.

Marina stood and raised her hands, water magic flowing through her with practiced ease. The air around Odion began to crystallize, moisture gathering and condensing until it formed a thin shell of ice around his body. Within moments, he was completely encased, looking like some strange sculpture preserved in crystal.

AURORA

The magical drain stopped immediately.

"How long do we have?" Hunter asked, staring at Odion's motionless form.

"Maybe ten minutes before hypothermia becomes a bigger threat than magical exhaustion," Marina replied, already moving to gather materials from her bag. "I need water—clean water—and these herbs."

She pulled out several small pouches that Hunter hadn't known she was carrying. Her hands moved with swift efficiency, mixing ingredients in a small metal cup and charging the mixture with her own magical energy.

"Where did you learn this?" Hunter asked, watching her work.

"My grandmother was a healer," Marina said without looking up. "She taught me that magical shock was like drowning—you have to restart the system gradually or you'll cause more damage."

Hunter found himself genuinely impressed by her competence. This wasn't the frightened prisoner he remembered from Aurora's basement or even the reluctant ally from their Rebellion days. They had never really worked together before, but he never really took her seriously before now. He couldn't have been more mistaken. This was someone who knew exactly what she was doing.

"I'm going to need you to melt the ice," Marina said, finishing her preparations. "But you have to do it slowly, starting from his heart outward. Too fast and the shock could kill him. Too slow and hypothermia will."

Hunter nodded, moving closer to the ice-encased Odion. "Just tell me what to do."

"Start with just a trickle of heat, right over his chest," Marina instructed, positioning herself with the remedy. "We need to warm his core first, then work outward."

Hunter placed his hands over Odion's heart, channeling the smallest amount of fire magic he could manage. It was like performing surgery with a blowtorch—requiring a level of control he rarely used. Sweat beaded on his forehead as he concentrated on keeping the heat gentle and even.

"Good," Marina murmured, carefully administering drops of her remedy as the ice around Odion's mouth melted. "Keep it steady."

As they worked together, the artificial barriers between them seemed to dissolve. There was no time for old grudges or political differences—only the shared goal of keeping Odion alive.

"Why did you really leave the Rebellion, Hunter?" Marina asked quietly, her voice focused but curious.

Hunter didn't take his eyes off his work, but his jaw tightened. "They wanted me to kill my best friend."

"Tobias," Marina said, understanding flooding her voice.

"I couldn't do it," Hunter admitted. "I know that makes me a traitor to you, but I couldn't murder someone I love just because Sabrina and Lucien told me to, to prove I'm loyal to them."

Marina was quiet for a moment, processing this. "I always wondered why you didn't just follow orders. You were loyal to the Rebellion for years."

"Loyalty has limits," Hunter replied, carefully melting the ice around Odion's arms. "At least mine does."

Gradually, color began to return to Odion's face. His breathing deepened and steadied. When the last of the ice melted away, he stirred, his eyes fluttering open.

"What happened?" he croaked, trying to sit up.

"Take it easy," Marina said, supporting him. "You overdid it with the teleportation. Drained an entire river trying to stay alive."

Odion looked around at the empty riverbed, his eyes widening in horror. "I did this?"

"It's not your fault," Hunter said quickly. "You pushed too hard, but we've all done that."

"I thought I could handle it," Odion said quietly, embarrassment clear in his voice. "I thought I was stronger than this."

Marina helped him to a sitting position. "Being strong doesn't mean ignoring your limits. It means knowing them and respecting them."

They set up a makeshift camp by the empty riverbed, none of them wanting to risk another teleportation attempt so soon. As they gathered firewood and prepared for the night, Marina pointed to the dead vegetation surrounding them.

"This kind of magical disturbance," she said thoughtfully, "the dead vegetation, the drained water sources... I've been tracking patterns like this for weeks."

Hunter looked up from the fire he was building. "The reports you mentioned. Aurora's done this too."

"But on a much larger scale," Marina added grimly. "If Odion could drain an entire river in one moment of crisis, imagine what Aurora could do over weeks or months of breakdown."

The implications hit Hunter like a physical blow. "She's destroying everything around her."

"And probably doesn't even realize it," Marina continued. "The patterns I've been tracking—they're getting stronger, more concentrated. She's somewhere remote, somewhere she can lose control without witnesses."

Odion struggled to his feet, still weak but determined. "We need to call Tobias. Tell him what happened, what we've figured out."

Hunter pulled out his phone, surprised to see he had signal despite their remote location. Tobias answered on the first ring.

"Hunter? Where are you? You're three hours late."

"We had some complications," Hunter said, glancing at Odion. "Odion pushed too hard on the teleportation and nearly died from magical exhaustion."

The silence on the other end of the line was deafening. When Tobias spoke again, his voice was tight with concern. "Is he okay? Are you both okay?"

"We're fine now, thanks to Marina," Hunter said, meeting her eyes across their small camp. "She saved his life, Toby. Knew exactly what to do."

"Marina." Tobias's voice carried a mixture of surprise and gratitude. "Thank you. Thank you for taking care of him."

"He's going to be fine," Marina said, leaning closer to the phone. "But we think we've figured out where Aurora might be. The magical disturbances I've been tracking—Odion's accident created the same pattern, just smaller."

"What kind of pattern?"

"Environmental destruction from uncontrolled magical drain," Hunter explained. "Aurora's probably somewhere remote, unconsciously pulling energy from everything around her to stay alive."

They talked for another few minutes, sharing what they'd learned and adjusting their plans. When Hunter hung up, the three of them sat around their small fire, the empty riverbed stretching out around them like a reminder of magic's true cost.

"I'm sorry," Odion said quietly. "For being so stubborn, for nearly getting us all killed."

"You weren't the only stubborn one," Hunter replied. "I pushed you to go faster when Marina was right to be cautious."

Marina poked at the fire with a stick, sending sparks dancing into the darkening sky. "We all learned something today. Maybe that's worth a dried-up river."

AURORA

"Tomorrow we'll take shorter jumps," Odion said. "Fifty miles at a time, with rest breaks between."

"Tomorrow we'll travel as a team," Hunter corrected. "No more lone wolf bullshit from any of us."

Marina smiled, the first genuinely warm expression Hunter had seen from her since they'd started traveling together. "I think I can live with that."

As they settled in for the night, Hunter found himself thinking about the conversation with Tobias. For the first time since Aurora had disappeared, they had a real lead on where she might be. But more than that, they had something Hunter hadn't expected to find: trust.

He looked over at Marina, who was checking on Odion's pulse one more time before sleep, and realized that somewhere between the crisis and the healing, they'd stopped being reluctant allies and become something else entirely.

Maybe even friends.

CHAPTER SIXTEEN:
Finding the Trail

The empty riverbed stretched out before them like a scar in the earth, the morning mist rising from the muddy crater where rushing water should have been. Odion stood at the edge of their makeshift camp, staring down at the devastation he'd caused, his shoulders tight with shame.

"I did this," he said quietly, his voice barely audible over the sound of Hunter breaking down their camp behind him. "An entire ecosystem, just... gone."

Marina appeared beside him, her blue hair catching the early morning light. "You were dying," she said simply. "Your magic did what it had to do to keep you alive."

"But look at it." Odion gestured helplessly at the barren wasteland. Dead fish lay scattered across the exposed riverbed like silver coins, their scales already dulling in the dawn air. The vegetation along what had once been the banks was withered and brown, crumbling at the slightest touch of wind.

"I've seen worse," Marina said, and something in her tone made Odion look at her sharply.

"Worse?"

"This is what I've been tracking for weeks," Marina explained, pulling a small notebook from her jacket pocket. "Aurora's been doing this same thing, but on a much larger scale. And for much longer."

Hunter approached with both their bags slung over his shoulder, his expression grim. "We need to get moving. The longer we stay here, the more questions someone might ask about why an entire river just disappeared overnight."

Odion nodded, though he still felt weak. His magic was slowly regenerating, but it would be hours before he was anywhere near full strength. The thought of attempting another teleportation so soon made his stomach turn.

"Fifty miles," Marina said firmly, reading his expression. "No more than fifty miles per jump, with rest breaks between. We're not risking another incident like yesterday."

"I can handle more than that," Odion protested, but his voice lacked conviction.

Hunter snorted. "Famous last words. Marina saved your life yesterday because you 'could handle it.' Maybe try listening to her this time."

Before they left, Hunter knelt beside a small puddle of remaining water, one of the few untouched by Odion's magical drain. "Let me try something first," he said, placing his palms flat on either side of the water.

The surface began to shimmer as Hunter focused his scrying magic into it. For a moment, images flickered across the water—flashes of trees, glimpses of mountains, fragments of a female figure. But the pictures were chaotic, shifting too rapidly to make sense of, like trying to watch television during a thunderstorm.

"Anything?" Marina asked hopefully.

Hunter shook his head, frustrated. "It's like trying to see through a storm. The images are too chaotic, too fragmented. Aurora's magical state is interfering with the scrying somehow."

Odion moved closer to the puddle, kneeling beside Hunter. "Let me try something different," he said, closing his eyes and extending his consciousness outward the way Aurora had taught him. Telepathic communication was difficult under the best circumstances, but maybe if he could just make contact...

He reached out with his mind, searching for any trace of Aurora's familiar presence. For long minutes he concentrated, sweat beading on his forehead despite the cool morning air. But there was nothing—complete silence where Aurora's thoughts should have been.

"Either she's too far away," Odion said finally, opening his eyes with disappointment, "or her mental state is too unstable for contact."

Marina was taking notes in her journal, documenting their failed attempts. "Then we do this the hard way," she said. "Through the water network."

Their first teleportation jump took them fifty miles southwest, landing them in a small clearing surrounded by pine trees. Odion managed it without incident, though he was breathing hard by the time they materialized.

"Rest break," Marina announced before either man could protest. "Fifteen minutes minimum."

As they caught their breath, Marina began explaining her tracking method. "Water magic lets me sense the health of water sources across long distances," she said, pulling out a detailed map marked with red X's. "It's like... imagine if you could taste every drop of water in a hundred-mile radius."

"That sounds overwhelming," Odion said, genuinely curious despite his exhaustion.

"Regular pollution would be," Marina agreed. "Industrial runoff, agricultural chemicals, even natural contamination—it's everywhere, and trying to track all of it would drive you insane. But magical contamination is different. It's rare enough to stand out, and it has a very specific signature."

She pointed to several marked locations on her map. "I've been systematically checking water sources for weeks, mapping every instance of magical contamination I could find. Most of it is minor—a stressed mage losing control for a few minutes, that kind of thing. But this..."

Marina traced a line through several of the red marks, creating a clear pattern heading northeast. "This is sustained, large-scale magical damage. The kind that only happens when someone is in serious breakdown for an extended period."

Hunter studied the map over her shoulder. "How do you know it's Aurora specifically?"

"Because I've felt her earth magic before," Marina said quietly, unconsciously touching her side where Aurora's thorns had once pierced her. "Every mage's magical signature is slightly different—like a fingerprint. Aurora's earth magic has a particular... intensity to it. When she loses control, it doesn't just drain life from plants. It corrupts the water they've absorbed, leaves traces in groundwater that can last for months."

She flipped to another page in her notebook, showing detailed readings and calculations. "Yesterday, when Odion nearly died, his magical drain created a signature almost identical to what I've been tracking. Same pattern, same type of environmental damage, just much smaller in scale."

"So, Aurora is out there somewhere, unconsciously destroying everything around her to stay alive," Odion said, the parallel to his own experience making him feel sick.

"For months," Marina confirmed grimly. "And the trail is leading toward some very remote mountain regions."

Their second jump took them another fifty miles, landing near a small town where Marina immediately headed for the nearest stream. She knelt beside the water, placing her hands just above the surface without quite touching it.

"Clean," she announced after a moment. "Whatever Aurora's doing, we're still outside the affected radius."

"How can you tell?" Hunter asked.

Marina's expression grew distant as she concentrated on her magic. "Healthy water has a certain... harmony to it. All the minerals and organic compounds are in proper balance. Magically contaminated water feels incompatible, like an orchestra where half the instruments are out of tune."

They continued their pattern of short jumps and rest breaks, with Marina checking water sources at each stop. As they traveled northeast, following the trail of contamination, she began finding traces of Aurora's magical signature.

"Getting a little stronger," she reported after their fourth jump. "We're definitely heading in the right direction."

During one of their rest stops, Marina and Odion found themselves sitting on a fallen log while Hunter scouted their next landing zone. The afternoon sun was warm on their faces, and for the first time since Odion's near-death experience, they had a moment of quiet conversation.

"I owe you my life," Odion said suddenly. "I haven't properly thanked you for what you did yesterday."

Marina waved off his gratitude. "You would have done the same for me."

"Would I?" Odion asked, genuine uncertainty in his voice. "I almost got us all killed because I was too proud to admit my limitations. Too anxious about disappointing Tobias to think clearly about the risks."

Marina studied his face, recognizing something familiar in his

AURORA

expression. "You always feel like you have to prove you belong, don't you?"

The accuracy of her observation hit Odion like a physical blow. "How did you...?"

"Because I do the same thing," Marina said simply. "Different methods, same anxiety. You push yourself too hard trying to prove you're capable. I obsess over details and planning trying to prove I'm valuable."

Odion was quiet for a moment, processing this. "Is that what the water tracking is about? Proving your worth to the team?"

Marina laughed, but there was no humor in it. "Partly. When everything feels out of control, I focus on what I can measure and map. It makes me feel useful, like I'm contributing something concrete instead of just being another problem to solve."

"But you are contributing," Odion protested. "Without your tracking method, we'd have no idea where to look for Aurora."

"And without your teleportation skills, we'd never get there in time to help her," Marina countered. "But we both know that's not really what this is about, is it?"

Odion sighed, recognizing the truth in her words. "I've always felt like I had to earn my place with the Bellwater Mages. Everyone else has years of experience, established relationships, proven abilities. I'm just the new guy who happened to stumble into their world."

"And I'm the former enemy who tortured their leader and tried to kill their friends," Marina said dryly. "Trust me, if anyone should feel like they don't belong, it's me."

They sat in comfortable silence for a few minutes, watching clouds drift across the sky. Finally, as Hunter rejoined them, Marina made a decision.

"I need to tell you both something," she said. "About why I've been so obsessive about this tracking. It's not just about proving I'm useful."

Both men turned their full attention to her.

"I keep seeing Aurora's face when she was torturing me," Marina said quietly. "Not angry or cruel, but... desperate. Terrified. Like she was drowning and taking it out on me because I was the only thing in reach. And I realize now that she was drowning. In guilt, in responsibility, in trying to hold everything together while falling apart inside."

She took a shaky breath. "I don't want to save Aurora because I forgive her or because I think she deserves it. I want to save her because I recognize that desperation. Because if we don't find her soon, she's going to destroy herself along with everything around her."

Hunter was staring at her with something approaching respect. "That's... actually the most honest thing anyone's said about this whole search."

"Tobias wants her back because he loves her," Marina continued. "You want to find her because Tobias asked you to, and you love him. Odion wants to help because it's the right thing to do. But me? I want to find her because I know what it's like to be drowning, and I know what it's like when no one throws you a lifeline."

Odion reached over and squeezed her shoulder gently. "For what it's worth, I'm glad you're here. Not just because your tracking abilities are saving our asses, but because... because I think Aurora's going to need someone who understands what she's been through."

"And because you saved my life," Odion added with a small smile. "Which means I owe you approximately forever."

Marina smiled back. "I'll settle for you not trying to teleport six hundred miles in one jump again."

"Deal," Odion laughed. "Though in my defense, I thought I could handle it."

"Famous last words," Hunter and Marina said in unison, making all three of them laugh.

AURORA

Their mood was considerably lighter as they continued their journey, the shared honesty having solidified something important between them. With each jump, Marina's readings grew a tiny bit stronger, confirming they were closing in on Aurora's location, though it was obvious they were still far away from her.

By evening, they had reached the outskirts of Bellwater. The familiar landscape felt strange after their day of travel, but also comforting. Aurora's cottage came into view as the sun was setting, warm light spilling from the windows.

Tobias was waiting for them on the front porch, and his relief at seeing them safe was visible from a hundred yards away. He practically ran to meet them, his eyes immediately checking Odion for signs of lingering injury.

"Thank God you're okay," he said, pulling Odion into a quick hug. "When Hunter called and said you'd nearly died…"

"I'm fine," Odion assured him. He felt his magical energy recharge a bit thanks to Tobias's hug and made a mental note that neither Hunter nor Marina hugged him to restore him to life. Not that it mattered; it was good to know there were other ways to restore one's magic. "Thanks entirely to Marina."

Tobias turned to Marina then, and the awkwardness was immediate. This was the woman Aurora had tortured, the person he'd struck with lightning during their escape. For a moment, neither of them seemed to know what to say.

"Marina," Tobias said finally, his voice heavy with sincerity. "I owe you an apology. For the lightning strike, for not stopping Aurora sooner, for everything you went through because of our failures. I'm sorry."

Marina blinked in surprise. Whatever she'd been expecting, it wasn't a genuine apology from the man she'd once considered an enemy.

"You saved Odion's life," Tobias continued. "After everything we put you through, you saved one of the people I care about most. I can never repay that."

"You don't need to repay anything," Marina said quietly. "We're on the same side now."

"Are we?" Tobias asked, and there was hope in his voice.

Marina nodded firmly. "We are." She looked at Hunter, who looked back at her, nodding; an unspoken agreement had been reached between the two former Arcane Rebellion members. If Sabrina and Lucien were ordering murder, then Marina couldn't be part of it either.

They moved inside, gathering around Aurora's kitchen table as Marina spread out her maps and notebooks. The evidence was overwhelming—weeks of careful tracking, detailed readings, undeniable patterns.

Marina concluded, pointing to her final calculations: "She's definitely somewhere in the remote mountain regions along the northern border. The magical contamination signature is consistent and strong."

Tobias stared at the map, running his hands through his hair. "Oh my God," he said slowly. "She really didn't want to be found, did she?"

"Or she wanted to make sure she couldn't hurt anyone else," Odion offered.

"Wait," Tobias said suddenly, studying Marina's map more closely. "This can't be right. She's in North Korea?!"

CHAPTER SEVENTEEN:
The Last Stand

Tobias had been awake since four in the morning, pacing Aurora's cottage with a cup of coffee that had long since gone cold. The team was supposed to arrive at eight. The meeting with Dr. Harrington was scheduled for eleven. Everything depended on having those three hours to coordinate their efforts, make their calls, and prepare their materials.

At 7:47 AM, his phone buzzed with a text from Beatrice: "Dr. Harrington here early with full team. Demands immediate meeting. Get here NOW."

The coffee mug slipped from Tobias's hands, shattering against the kitchen floor in a spray of ceramic and cold caffeine. Three hours had just become zero hours.

He was in his car and racing toward the school before his conscious mind had fully processed what was happening. His phone rang as he pulled into the Bellwater Academy parking lot—Hunter, calling from somewhere on the road.

"Toby, we're still twenty minutes out—"

"She's here," Tobias said, his voice tight with panic. "Dr. Harrington arrived early. The meeting's happening now."

Silence on the other end, then Hunter's voice, grim: "What do you need us to do?"

"Everything. All at once. While I try to stall her." Tobias was already walking toward the school entrance, his mind racing through impossible logistics. "Hunter, you need to get to that basement immediately. The physical evidence has to be dealt with before she decides to take another look."

"On it."

"Foxton, Finnian—are you listening?"

"We're here, Mr. T," Foxton's voice came through the speaker, tense but determined.

"Donor calls. Now. We need commitments, not just promises. Real money, real numbers I can present in there."

"Already pulling up the database," Finnian's voice, steady as always.

"Odion, Marina—"

"Administrative support and new teacher credentials," Odion interrupted. "We've got it. How long can you stall?"

Tobias paused at the school's front door, looking through the glass at Dr. Harrington's imposing figure in the main hallway, surrounded by her team of investigators. "I have no idea," he admitted.

The front office felt like walking into a war zone. Dr. Harrington stood near Beatrice's desk with three other officials, their briefcases and tablets spread across every available surface. The air crackled with administrative authority and barely contained impatience.

"Mr. Thornfield," Dr. Harrington said, her voice carrying the crisp edge of someone whose time had been wasted. "I trust you're prepared for our final evaluation?"

"Of course," Tobias replied, forcing his voice to remain steady. "Though I have to admit, I wasn't expecting you quite this early."

"Early completion of our preliminary reviews allowed us to accelerate the timeline," she said, gesturing to her team. "I see no reason to delay when we can resolve this matter immediately."

Tobias's heart stopped for just a second before he composed himself. "Naturally. I just need a few minutes to gather our materials—"

"The materials you've had forty-eight hours to prepare?" Dr. Harrington's eyebrow arched with skeptical authority.

Behind her, Beatrice caught Tobias's eye and gave the slightest of nods. Then she turned to her computer with the deliberate movements of someone about to be very, very helpful.

"Dr. Harrington," Beatrice said sweetly, "before we begin, I should mention that state regulation 847-B requires you to review the complete meeting minutes from our school board sessions over the past year. For transparency and compliance purposes."

Dr. Harrington paused, clearly annoyed but unable to argue with official procedure. "How extensive are these minutes?"

Beatrice's fingers clicked across her keyboard with practiced efficiency. "Let me print those for you right now. It's... eight hundred and two pages. Single-spaced, as per state archival requirements."

The printer in the corner immediately began its laborious work, mechanical sounds that felt like salvation to Tobias's ears. Dr. Harrington's expression suggested she was beginning to understand that this morning might not proceed as efficiently as she'd hoped.

"While those are printing," Tobias said quickly, "let me gather the financial projections and staffing documentation you requested. Perhaps we could start with a general overview in the conference room?"

Twenty minutes later, Tobias sat across from Dr. Harrington in Bellwater Academy's small conference room, a stack of 802 pages of meeting minutes between them like a paper fortress. His phone buzzed constantly with updates from his team, each text message feeling like a lifeline.

Hunter: "Basement cleared. Working on evidence alterations."

Finnian: "Three donors confirmed. Working on two more."

Odion: "ETA 10 minutes with full administrative package."

"Mr. Thornfield," Dr. Harrington said, looking up from her methodical review of the meeting minutes, "I notice several references to budgetary concerns in these documents. Specifically, mentions of 'irregular funding sources' and 'non-traditional revenue streams.'"

Tobias's heart hammered against his ribs. "Those references relate to our grant applications and private donor relationships," he said carefully. "We've been working to diversify our funding base to ensure long-term stability."

"Private donors," Dr. Harrington repeated, making a note. "I'll need to see a complete list of these donors, along with contribution records and contact information."

"Absolutely," Tobias replied, praying that Foxton and Finnian were making progress. "I'm having those records compiled now."

His phone buzzed: Foxton: "Five major donors confirmed. $47,000 in immediate commitments. Still working."

Relief flooded through Tobias's chest, but he kept his expression neutral. "In fact, I should have those donor records within the next few minutes."

Dr. Harrington flipped to another page of meeting minutes, her expression growing more puzzled. "Mr. Thornfield, I'm seeing repeated references to something called 'special education services for displaced students.' Can you elaborate on these programs?"

"Certainly," Tobias said, though his mind was racing. Those references were Aurora's coded language for magical training. How could he explain them without revealing the truth? "We've been providing enhanced support services for students who've experienced significant trauma. Individualized attention, specialized counseling, that sort of thing."

"And the staff qualifications for these specialized services?"

Tobias's phone buzzed again: Agatha: "Documentation ready. Matilda and I have everything prepared."

"Our staff transition documents will outline those qualifications," Tobias said. "I believe my colleagues are finalizing those materials now."

Dr. Harrington set down the meeting minutes with a slight frown. "Mr. Thornfield, I appreciate your cooperation, but I'm growing concerned about the number of materials that are still being 'finalized' for a meeting you've had forty-eight hours to prepare for."

Before Tobias could respond, there was a soft knock on the conference room door. Agatha entered, moving carefully on her crutches but carrying herself with the dignity of someone who had been handling administrative crises since before Dr. Harrington was born.

"Forgive the interruption," Agatha said with old-fashioned courtesy, "but I have the staffing transition documentation you requested."

She placed a neatly organized folder on the table, followed immediately by Matilda, who carried additional binders with professional efficiency.

"Dr. Harrington," Agatha continued, "I'm Agatha O'Connor, senior English teacher. This is Matilda Carrington, our special education coordinator. We've prepared comprehensive explanations for the recent staff departures, along with transition plans and replacement procedures."

Dr. Harrington accepted the materials with obvious interest. "These departures were rather sudden, weren't they?"

"Life rarely follows administrative timelines," Agatha replied with dry humor. "Ms. Braithwaite received an unexpected job offer from a prestigious university. Mr. Rodson had a family emergency that required immediate relocation. Ms. Wildwood... well, Ms. Wildwood had been showing signs of significant stress for some time. Her departure, while sudden, was not entirely surprising to those of us who worked closely with her."

"What kind of stress?" Dr. Harrington asked, leaning forward with interest.

Matilda and Agatha exchanged a glance that spoke of years of professional collaboration. "The kind that manifests as increasingly erratic decision-making," Matilda said carefully. "Difficulty delegating responsibilities, conflicts with colleagues, communication breakdowns with important stakeholders."

"In other words," Agatha added, "the kind of leadership crisis that was becoming detrimental to institutional stability."

Tobias watched in amazement as the two teachers systematically dismantled any narrative of Aurora as an indispensable leader. They weren't lying; every word they spoke was technically true, but they were reframing Aurora's departure as a positive development rather than a catastrophic loss.

"And you have replacement candidates?" Dr. Harrington asked.

"We do indeed," Tobias said, as his phone buzzed with another update: Odion: "Arriving now with Marina and Hunter. Full credentials package ready."

Five minutes later, the conference room had transformed into something resembling a job fair. Odion spread administrative documents across the table with the efficient precision of someone who understood bureaucratic expectations. Marina sat beside him with a calm professionalism that somehow made her vivid blue hair seem like an asset rather than a distraction.

Hunter entered last, and Tobias held his breath until he saw the subtle thumbs-up gesture that meant the basement evidence had been successfully handled.

"Dr. Harrington," Tobias said, feeling genuine confidence for the first time all morning, "I'd like to introduce our new faculty members. Hunter Diaz will be joining us as our science teacher, and Marina Torres as our arts and music instructor."

Dr. Harrington studied both candidates with the skeptical attention of someone who had seen too many desperate hiring decisions. "Your qualifications?"

Hunter pulled out a folder of documents that looked remarkably official for something that had been assembled in a moving car. "Master's degree in chemistry from UC Berkeley, five years of teaching experience in public and private institutions. Letters of recommendation from three previous principals."

Marina's credentials were equally impressive. "BFA in studio arts from Portland State, with additional certification in music education. Experience in both traditional classroom settings and therapeutic arts programs."

"Therapeutic arts programs?" Dr. Harrington asked, clearly intrigued.

"Art and music therapy for students who've experienced trauma," Marina explained smoothly. "Given your school's population of displaced students, I thought those skills might be particularly valuable."

Tobias watched Dr. Harrington's expression shift from skepticism to interest. Marina was positioning herself as exactly what Bellwater Academy needed: someone who could address the specialized needs that had made their student population seem problematic to outside observers.

His phone buzzed one final time: Foxton. "Eight donors confirmed. $73,000 committed. Financial crisis officially solved."

"Dr. Harrington," Tobias said, pulling out his own folder of documents, "I have the financial information you requested. Complete donor list, contribution records, and immediate commitments that address our short-term budgetary concerns."

She reviewed the materials with the thorough attention of someone who understood that numbers don't lie. As she read, Tobias felt the atmosphere in the room shifting from crisis management to genuine institutional planning.

"Mr. Thornfield," Dr. Harrington said finally, setting down the financial projections, "this is... quite impressive. You've managed to secure significant funding commitments in a very short timeframe."

"Our donor relationships are strong," Tobias replied, which was now technically true thanks to Foxton and Finnian's morning of intensive phone calls. "The recent communication gaps were unfortunate, but easily remedied with proper attention."

Dr. Harrington stood and walked to the window, looking out at the school grounds with an expression Tobias couldn't quite read. When she turned back to face the group, her official demeanor had softened slightly.

"I'll be honest with you," she said. "When I began this investigation, I expected to find an institution in complete administrative collapse. Financial mismanagement, leadership chaos, safety concerns that put students at risk."

She gestured to the materials spread across the conference table. "What I'm seeing instead is a school that has faced significant challenges but is responding with competent leadership and concrete solutions. The basement issues you've addressed, the financial commitments you've secured, the quality of your replacement staff...these suggest an institution that's not just surviving its difficulties, but learning from them."

Tobias felt something like hope beginning to bloom in his chest, though he tried not to let it show too obviously.

"That said," Dr. Harrington continued, "there will be conditions. Quarterly financial reporting for the next two years. Surprise inspections to ensure continued compliance. And I'll want to see evidence of improved communication with your donor base."

"Absolutely," Tobias said immediately. "Whatever oversight you deem necessary."

"Additionally, I'll need written confirmation that Ms. Wildwood will not be returning to any administrative capacity at this institution. Her departure appears to have been beneficial for everyone involved."

The words hit Tobias like a physical blow, though he managed to keep his expression neutral. "I can provide that confirmation," he said quietly.

Dr. Harrington nodded with satisfaction. "In that case, Mr. Thornfield, I'm prepared to recommend that Bellwater Academy remain open, subject to the conditions I've outlined. Congratulations. You've managed to save your school."

The meeting concluded with handshakes and administrative details, but Tobias barely heard the specifics. They'd done it. Against impossible odds, with no time to prepare, they'd actually done it.

As Dr. Harrington and her team packed up their materials and headed for the exit, Tobias found himself alone in the conference room with his friends and colleagues. The silence stretched for a long moment before Foxton broke it.

"Did we actually just pull that off?"

"We did," Odion said, sinking into one of the conference chairs with obvious exhaustion. "Though I'm not sure I ever want to experience anything that stressful again."

"The kids on the phone calls were amazing," Finnian added. "Once we explained what was at stake, they couldn't contribute fast enough. Turns out a lot of people have been wanting to help but didn't know how."

Agatha tapped her crutch against the floor with satisfaction. "Forty years of dealing with bureaucrats finally paid off. Though I have to say, Aurora made it rather easy to present her departure as a positive development."

The comment created an uncomfortable silence. Marina was the one who finally addressed what everyone was thinking.

"What happens when she comes back?" she asked quietly.

Tobias looked around the room at the people who had just saved their community. Hunter and Marina, former enemies who had proven themselves as allies; Foxton and Finnian, students who had shown remarkable maturity and capability; Agatha and Matilda, veteran teachers who had stepped up when everything was falling apart; Odion, who had become the friend and colleague Tobias had never expected to find.

"When Aurora comes back," Tobias said slowly, "she'll find a school that doesn't need saving. She'll find a community that's learned to work together without her. And maybe…" He paused, trying to find words for something he'd never articulated before. "Maybe that will be better for everyone."

Hunter nodded thoughtfully. "Including her."

CHAPTER EIGHTEEN:
Borrowed Time

The evening light filtering through Bellwater Cottage's windows felt different somehow; warmer, more welcoming than it had in months. Tobias stood in the kitchen, still wearing his rumpled dress shirt from the morning's crisis, staring at the simple spread Agatha and Matilda had brought: a pot of Irish stew that smelled like home, fresh bread still warm from the oven, and a collection of mismatched bowls and plates that somehow made everything feel more genuine.

"I still can't believe we pulled that off," Foxton said for the third time, collapsing into one of Aurora's kitchen chairs with the boneless exhaustion of someone who'd been running on adrenaline for hours. His red hair was sticking up at odd angles, and there were ink stains on his fingers from all the note-taking he'd done during the donor calls.

"Believe it," Finnian replied, carefully arranging napkins with the methodical precision that characterized everything he did. "We had solid data, clear objectives, and excellent execution. The outcome was actually quite predictable once we implemented proper coordination."

Odion snorted from his position by the window, where he'd been keeping watch out of habit more than necessity. "Leave it to Finnian to make saving our entire world sound like a successful science experiment."

"It kind of was a science experiment," Hunter pointed out, settling into his chair with obvious relief. The day's stress had left visible marks on all of them, but Hunter looked particularly drained. "We had a hypothesis that we could convince Dr. Harrington the school was viable. We tested it with evidence and documentation. We got the results we wanted."

Foxton and Finnian glanced at the man, and Tobias realized that they hadn't really spent much time with him since he had burned down their school. Their looks of shock, suspicion, and fear were to be expected. Hunter didn't seem to notice. Tobias frowned and looked around some more.

Marina sat quietly at the far end of the table, her vivid blue hair pulled back in a simple ponytail. She'd been invited to this celebration, but Tobias could see she still felt uncertain about her place in it. The transition from enemy to ally was never easy, and Marina was still finding her footing with people who had every reason not to trust her.

"Marina," Agatha said, ladling stew into bowls with the efficient movements of someone who'd fed countless people over the years, "that performance as our new arts teacher was absolutely brilliant. Where on earth did you learn to sound so... pedagogically professional?"

Marina's cheeks colored slightly. "My grandmother was a teacher. I spent a lot of time listening to her talk about curriculum development and therapeutic methodologies." She paused, then added quietly, "I never thought I'd use that knowledge to help save a school."

"Well, you did," Matilda said airily, passing around the warm bread. "And we're grateful for it. All of us."

The simple statement seemed to settle something in Marina's expression. She accepted her bowl of stew with a small smile that transformed her entire face.

They ate in comfortable quiet for a while, the stress of the morning gradually giving way to something Tobias hadn't felt in months: peace. Not the desperate calm before a storm, but actual peace. The kind that came from knowing, at least for tonight, that everyone was safe.

"You know what I keep thinking about?" Foxton said, breaking the silence. "Those donor calls. Some of those people had been waiting for months just for someone to call them back. Mrs. Trias said she'd written three letters asking how she could help more, and no one ever responded!"

Finnian nodded grimly. "Aurora's communication breakdown was more extensive than we realized. We found seventeen families who'd been trying to increase their donations but couldn't get through to anyone."

"Seventeen families," Tobias repeated, feeling a familiar twist of guilt in his stomach. How had he not known about this? How had he missed something so fundamental to their survival?

"Hey," Hunter said, apparently reading his expression. "Don't start that self-blame spiral, Toby. Aurora kept all of us in the dark about the financial situation. You can't fix problems you don't know exist."

"Hunter's right," Odion agreed. "And more importantly, look what happened when people finally got accurate information. Seventeen families who wanted to help more. That tells us something important about our community."

"It tells us we have real support," Matilda said thoughtfully. "Not just financial support, but people who genuinely care about what we're doing here. That's... that's actually pretty remarkable."

Agatha raised her mug of coffee in a mock toast. "To the miracle of competent communication. May we never again mistake bureaucratic neglect for intentional policy."

Everyone laughed, and the sound filled the cottage with something it had been missing for too long: genuine joy. Not the brittle happiness of people trying to convince themselves everything was fine, but the real thing.

The kind that came from shared accomplishment and mutual respect.

Tobias set down his empty bowl, considering his words carefully. He knew he needed to address this, and now was as good a time as any. "When Aurora comes back," he said slowly, "she'll find a school that doesn't need constant crisis management. She'll find a community that's learned to work together without someone micromanaging every decision."

"Will that be good for her?" Foxton asked quietly. "I mean, if her whole identity is built around being the person who holds everything together..."

"That's exactly why it will be good for her," Tobias said firmly. "Aurora's been carrying weight that was never meant to be carried by one person. Maybe seeing that we can function without her constant oversight will help her realize she doesn't have to be responsible for everyone and everything."

"Or it might devastate her," Odion said gently. "People who define themselves through being needed don't always respond well to discovering they're not indispensable."

Marina was washing dishes at the sink, but Tobias could tell she was listening intently to every word. Finally, she spoke without turning around.

"When I was being... when Aurora was interrogating me, she kept saying things like 'I have to protect him' and 'It's my responsibility to keep him safe.' Never 'I want to help him' or 'I care about him.' Always obligation, always duty." Marina turned to face the group, her hands still dripping dishwater. "That's not love. That's obsession with control."

The brutal honesty of Marina's observation hit them all like cold water. No one argued with her assessment, because they'd all seen it. Aurora's fierce protectiveness that sometimes looked more like possession than affection.

"So, what do we do when she comes back?" Finnian asked practically.

"We show her who we've become," Tobias said. "We show her that we can be a team instead of followers. And we hope that's something she can learn to be part of."

AURORA

"And if it's not?" Foxton pressed.

Tobias looked around at the faces of people who had become more than colleagues: they'd become family. "Then we'll deal with that too. Together."

As the evening wound down and people began to leave, Tobias found himself alone in Aurora's cottage—no, not Aurora's cottage, his cottage--for the first time since the crisis had started. The familiar space felt different now, not like Aurora's domain temporarily vacated, but like a neutral space that belonged to all of them.

He settled into Aurora's favorite chair, looking out at the garden she'd tended so carefully. Even in the fading light, he could see the signs of her attention: carefully pruned roses, herb gardens arranged with mathematical precision, flower beds that bloomed in perfect seasonal succession.

Tobias allowed himself to really think about Aurora without the crushing weight of immediate crisis. Not Aurora the missing leader or Aurora the liability, but Aurora the person. The woman who had saved his life when he'd tried to end it. The friend who had stood by him through his darkest periods. The colleague whose dedication to their mission had never wavered, even when her methods had become problematic.

She was still out there somewhere, probably suffering, possibly dying. And despite everything, the violence, the control, the damage she'd caused, he still loved her. Not the desperate, grateful love of someone who owed her his life, but the complicated, enduring love of someone who had known her for years and understood both her best and worst qualities.

When she came back—and he was certain she would come back—things would be different. They'd all be different. The question was whether different would be better, or whether it would simply be a new kind of difficult.

Tobias pulled out his phone and scrolled through his contacts until he found Marina's number. After a moment's hesitation, he typed a message: "Thank you for everything today. And thank you for your honesty about Aurora. We needed to hear that."

Her response came back quickly: "Thank you for including me. I know it wasn't easy."

"You earned your place today. You're part of this now, for as long as you want to be."

"I want to be."

Tobias smiled, setting his phone aside. They'd faced their worst crisis and emerged stronger. They'd built something together that was more resilient than what they'd had before. Whatever challenges Aurora's return might bring, they would face them as a team.

For tonight, that was enough.

Two weeks later, Tobias stood in the security line at Dulles International Airport, trying to look like just another traveler heading off on spring break. The cover story they'd developed was simple: educational research trip to study Korean history and culture. Academic enough to justify the travel, boring enough that most people wouldn't ask follow-up questions.

"Documents," the security agent said without looking up.

Tobias handed over his passport and boarding pass, forcing himself to appear calm despite the nervous energy coursing through his system. Behind him in line, he could hear Odion explaining to another agent that the laptop in his bag contained "research materials and travel itineraries." Hunter and Marina were several people back, maintaining the careful distance they'd agreed upon to avoid looking like a coordinated group.

The weeks since saving the school had passed in a blur of careful planning and preparation. Marina's water-tracking had provided increasingly precise coordinates for Aurora's location, narrowing it down to a specific region in the mountains along the North Korean border. The plan was complex but straightforward: fly to Seoul, travel north under the guise of historical research, then cross into North Korea through one of the less monitored border areas that Hunter's old Rebellion contacts had identified.

AURORA

It was dangerous, probably illegal, and definitely not something any of them should be attempting without proper government authorization. But Aurora was running out of time. Marina's readings suggested the environmental damage around her was accelerating, which meant her magical breakdown was getting worse.

They couldn't wait for proper channels or diplomatic solutions. Aurora needed them now.

"Purpose of your visit to South Korea?" the customs official asked when Tobias reached the front of the line.

"Educational research," Tobias replied smoothly. "I'm a teacher studying Korean historical sites for a curriculum development project."

The official stamped his passport with perfunctory efficiency and waved him through. One hurdle cleared.

The international terminal buzzed with the controlled chaos of people from dozens of countries all trying to get somewhere else. Tobias made his way toward their gate, checking his phone for updates from the rest of his team. Everyone had cleared security without incident. Marina's equipment—disguised as standard research instruments—had passed inspection. Hunter's carefully forged documentation had held up to scrutiny.

So far, so good.

Tobias bought coffee at a small café near their gate, using the purchase as an excuse to survey the waiting area. A handful of business travelers typed on laptops. A young couple shared earbuds while watching something on a tablet. An elderly man read a Korean-language newspaper with intense concentration.

Normal airport scene. Nothing suspicious. Nothing to worry about.

He was settling into a seat with his coffee when Odion appeared beside him, looking pale despite his attempts to appear casual.

"Toby," Odion said quietly, not quite sitting down. "We have a problem."

"What kind of problem?"

Instead of answering, Odion nodded toward the far end of the gate area. "Look."

Tobias followed his gaze and felt his blood turn to ice water.

There, sitting calmly in the departure lounge as if they belonged there, were Sabrina Braithwaite and Lucien Rodson.

CHAPTER NINETEEN:
Restoration

Aurora woke to the sound of water running. Not the familiar trickle of the mountain stream that had become her morning soundtrack, but something different—the steady, purposeful flow of water that had somewhere to go. She sat up in her cot, listening intently. It took her a moment to realize what she was hearing: snowmelt, rushing down the mountainside in rivulets and streams as winter finally began its retreat.

She jumped as Raven sat down next to her.

"Jeez…give a girl a heart attack, why don't you?!"

Raven grinned sheepishly at her. "You're fine. You're young. What are you doing?"

"Listening to the snow melt."

"An interesting pastime. Some might call it boring. Like watching paint dry."

Aurora chuckled as she thought about what a normal person would think of her response. She supposed Raven had a point; it was kind of an unusual way to spend time.

"Of course, we who study the ways of the Earth know that there's much to be learned from listening to snow melt," Raven continued seriously, as though she hadn't just made a sarcastic joke.

Aurora nodded. "I know. I…the Earth is hurting. I can feel it. I don't know how to describe it, but…I can just feel it."

Aurora turned to look at the indigenous Elder that she had grown to respect, to admire, to love even.

"I want to see it."

"See what?"

"The damage I did when I first arrived in this beautiful place."

"Now child, why would you want to see a thing like that?"

"I can't keep hiding from what I've done. And if I'm really getting better, if I'm really learning to control my magic… maybe I can start making amends."

Raven looked at the young, strong black woman whom she had grown to idolize. Then she nodded.

"Okay."

They walked together through the forest that surrounded Raven's shelter, following paths that Aurora remembered only dimly from her weeks of breakdown. The snow was patchy now, revealing dead grass and withered undergrowth where her magic had drained the life from everything in reach. But there were other signs too; tiny flowers and grass pushing through the brown earth, early wildflowers that had somehow survived her magical rampage.

When they reached the clearing where Aurora had first collapsed, she stopped short. The devastation was worse than she'd remembered. A circle of dead trees stretched out in every direction, their branches bare and brittle as old bones. The stream that had once run clear and bright was a stagnant pool of murky water, lifeless and still.

AURORA

"I did this," Aurora said quietly, her voice carrying shame but not the self-hatred that had once consumed her. "I poisoned an entire ecosystem because I couldn't handle my own pain."

"Yes," Raven agreed simply. "You did."

Aurora walked to the edge of the dead stream, kneeling beside the contaminated water. She could feel the magical toxins she'd left behind, a sour corruption that made her stomach turn. But she could also feel something else; her own magic, responding not with chaos but with purpose.

"I need to fix it," she said, placing her hands just above the water's surface. "I don't know if I can, but I need to try."

"Earth magic isn't just about combat and control," Raven said, settling beside her. "It's about balance. About working with natural systems instead of imposing your will on them."

Aurora closed her eyes, extending her magical awareness into the poisoned water. It was delicate work, requiring a level of precision she'd never learned at Bellwater Academy. Instead of forcing change, she had to coax it. Instead of commanding the water to be clean, she had to gently extract the corruption she'd left behind.

Slowly, carefully, Aurora began to draw the magical toxins out of the water. It felt completely different from destructive magic, less like wielding a weapon and more like performing surgery. She had to separate her own magical signature from the natural minerals and organic compounds, pulling out only what didn't belong.

"That's it," Raven murmured encouragingly. "Feel the difference between your magic and the water's natural state. You're not controlling it, you're healing it."

The work was exhausting in a way Aurora hadn't expected. Destructive magic had always been easy, immediate, satisfying in its power. This healing magic required patience, sustained focus, and a level of humility she was still learning. But as she worked, she began to see results. The murky water grew clearer. The stagnant pool began to move again, finding its way back to the natural flow patterns she'd disrupted.

After what felt like hours, Aurora opened her eyes to see clear water running over smooth stones. As she watched, a small fish swam past, the first sign of returning life.

"How did you learn this?" Aurora asked, her voice thick with wonder.

"The same way you're learning it now," Raven replied. "By making mistakes and then choosing to fix them instead of running away."

They spent the morning working through other damaged areas around the shelter. Aurora learned to channel life energy into withered plants, watching in amazement as new buds appeared on branches she'd thought were permanently dead. She discovered that her earth magic had always been more powerful than she'd known. Bellwater's combat-focused training had only taught her a fraction of what she was capable of.

"I could have been healing people instead of just protecting them," Aurora said as she coaxed new growth from a tree that had been reduced to a skeletal trunk. "All those years, and I never learned that protection and healing are different skills."

"Different skills, same heart," Raven corrected gently. "You were always trying to help people. You just had limited tools."

By afternoon, Aurora was working for hours without any magical instability. Her magic responded to conscious intention rather than emotional triggers, flowing where she directed it instead of lashing out chaotically. When a butterfly landed on a flower she'd just restored to health, Aurora felt something she hadn't experienced in months: pure joy, uncomplicated by guilt or fear.

AURORA

"You know," Raven said casually as they took a break beside the now-clear stream, "I saw a sunflower blooming down the mountain yesterday. First one of the season."

Aurora felt the comment register in her mind—sunflower, Elena, the attack—but instead of the usual spike of panic, she simply felt sad. "I hope it's in a place where it can grow safely," she said softly. "Sunflowers deserve better than to be turned into weapons."

Raven smiled with satisfaction. "Indeed, they do."

As the sun began to set, they made their way back to the shelter. Aurora looked over her shoulder at the restoration work they'd accomplished. Clear water running in its proper channels, new growth emerging from dead soil, the first signs of an ecosystem beginning to heal itself.

"You've learned to use your magic as a tool rather than a weapon," Raven observed as they settled into their evening routine.

Aurora felt quiet pride in the visible results of her efforts. She'd repaired damage instead of causing it, healed instead of harmed.

"Raven," she said as they prepared their dinner, "I've been thinking about what comes next. About the memories I still haven't been able to face properly."

Raven looked up from her cooking, her expression growing serious. "Tell me what you're thinking."

"Today I learned that restoration work is possible. That I can take something I destroyed and help it heal." Aurora met Raven's eyes steadily. "If I can restore what I destroyed out there, maybe I can face what I destroyed in there."

She gestured to her head, and they both knew she was talking about Elena's terrified face, about the police officers falling in the earthquake, about all the people who had suffered because of her loss of control.

"Those are big memories, Aurora," Raven warned gently. "The skills you used today—organizing chaos into order—are exactly what you need. But facing Elena's attack, the police massacre... that will be the most difficult work yet."

Aurora nodded, feeling the truth of that in her bones. But she also felt something else: the realization that thinking about those memories no longer caused her magic to panic. They were still painful, still overwhelming, but her magic remained steady even as she contemplated them.

"I'm not ready to be happy about what I did," Aurora said slowly. "I don't think I ever will be. But I think I'm ready to face it without drowning in it."

"The restoration work was preparation," Raven said. "Now we tackle what you haven't been able to face."

"I owe it to her," Aurora said quietly. "I owe it to all of them. If I'm really healing, if I'm really becoming someone who can be trusted with power again, then I need to face everything I've done."

Raven studied her, then nodded. "Tomorrow morning, we'll work with the Elena memory. But Aurora—this will be unlike anything we've done so far. These memories have weight that will try to crush you."

"I know," Aurora replied. "But if true healing means facing everything, not just the manageable pieces, then that's what I need to do."

CHAPTER TWENTY:
The Price of Clarity

"That memory has fought back every time we've approached it," Raven warned, moving to arrange her memory stones in a more complex pattern than Aurora had ever seen. She added extra protective barriers, created additional safeguards. "Some memories don't want to be organized. They want to stay exactly as sharp and painful as when they first formed."

"I owe it to her," Aurora said firmly. "I need to see her face clearly, without my own guilt distorting what happened. If I can't face this, then all the other healing work is meaningless."

Raven completed her preparations, then settled across from Aurora with an expression of deep concern. "Sometimes clarity is more painful than confusion," she said quietly. "Are you certain you're ready for that?"

Aurora could avoid this memory forever. She could return to Bellwater having organized every trauma except this one, could spend the rest of her life carefully stepping around the moment she'd demonstrated exactly what kind of teacher she really was.

"I'm ready," she said, settling into the cross-legged position that had become second nature.

Aurora closed her eyes and let the memory come.

She was back in the clearing behind Bellwater Cottage, teaching the students who had lost everything. The lesson had not been going well—she'd been demonstrating the emotional foundations of magic, showing them how feelings could be channeled into growth, but the children just didn't seem to be all that interested. She remembered, vaguely, a comment that had been made about them not wanting to study magic prior to the lesson. All the same, three perfect sunflowers had bloomed in her palm, bright and beautiful examples of magic's creative potential.

Then Elena had asked her question, the one that had changed everything.

"But isn't magic supposed to be a weapon? What good's a sunflower in a fight if we're fighting against fire?"

Not sarcasm. Not mockery. A legitimate tactical question from a girl who had watched her friends burn and wanted to know if the magic Aurora was teaching could actually protect people.

But Aurora had heard dismissal. She'd heard this traumatized child questioning whether Aurora's magic was weak, decorative, useless. And in that instant, Aurora had decided to teach Elena exactly what sunflowers could do.

The attack had been calculated, deliberate. Aurora had made the sunflower leap from her hand to Elena's throat with conscious intent, squeezing tighter and tighter as the girl struggled for breath. Not a moment of lost control, a demonstration of power designed to humiliate and terrify.

Elena's face had turned blue as she clawed at the supernatural noose. Lyra had screamed and tried to pull the flower away, only making it squeeze tighter. Darian had shouted for Aurora to stop. Foxton and Finnian had stood frozen in horror.

And Aurora had let it continue. Had watched this child suffocate while making her point about the deadliness of "pretty flowers." Only when

AURORA

Elena was seconds from unconsciousness had Aurora finally released the spell, watching with satisfaction as the girl collapsed, gasping and sobbing.

"I think that will conclude our lesson for today," Aurora had said with cold authority. "Please mind what insults you give me and my plants in the future."

The memory played out with devastating clarity. Aurora could see now that Elena's question hadn't been an insult at all. It had been the desperate inquiry of a girl trying to understand if the magic being offered could prevent another Jefferson High.

"I nearly murdered a child for asking if I could actually protect her," Aurora whispered, her voice thick with horror.

But this time, something was different. The memory remained vivid and painful, but Aurora's magic stayed completely stable. No tremors, no chaotic outpouring of earth magic, no desperate drain on the environment around her. She could see the attack clearly, like watching a film of someone else.

Working with the same methodical precision she'd used for the restoration work, Aurora began separating the different threads of the memory. Elena's legitimate concern about combat applications went into one mental folder. Aurora's wounded pride and need to demonstrate dominance went into another folder, properly labeled and contained. The calculated cruelty itself, the decision to terrorize a traumatized child to make a point, went into a third file.

Each thread was organized, catalogued, filed away where it could inform her future choices without controlling her present state.

"I can see it all now," Aurora said, opening her eyes to find Raven watching her with amazement. "The memory... it doesn't own me anymore."

"You've mastered the technique," Raven said with genuine pride. "That was the hardest possible test, and you passed. You've learned to carry trauma without being controlled by it."

Aurora stood and walked outside, needing air and space to process what she'd accomplished. The successful organization of Elena's attack should have felt like triumph. She could return to Bellwater now, could face Elena and make proper amends, could rebuild the relationships she'd damaged.

So why did she feel like the world was ending?

The answer came with crystal clarity as Aurora looked out over the forest she'd been healing. Without trauma clouding her judgment, she could finally see her entire relationship with Tobias for what it really was.

Every time Tobias had voiced concerns or objections, Aurora had found ways to silence him. When he'd hesitated about substitute teaching, she'd worn down his resistance with guilt and obligation. When he'd expressed doubts about Aurora's methods, she'd questioned his loyalty and commitment. When he'd tried to make his own decisions, she'd found ways to prove he needed her guidance.

The sunflower attack wasn't an anomaly. It had been the most visible example of who she'd always been, someone who used power to punish anyone who questioned her authority.

"I treated him exactly the same way I treated Elena," Aurora said aloud, her voice hollow with realization. "Different methods, same fundamental disrespect for his autonomy."

Aurora sank to her knees beside the restored stream, watching clear water flow over smooth stones. Her healing work here had been successful because she'd learned to work with natural systems instead of imposing her will on them. But with Tobias, she'd spent years imposing her will on every aspect of his life, just more subtly than she'd done with Elena.

Even now, even with all her healing and growth, Aurora could feel the familiar patterns waiting just beneath the surface. The need to know where he was, what he was doing, whether he was making good choices. The urge to guide his decisions, to protect him from options she didn't approve of.

"I love Tobias," she whispered to the running water. "But... I can't love him the way he deserves."

Raven appeared beside her, settling on the bank with the patience of someone who had walked this path before.

"You're understanding something important," Raven said gently.

"You told me once not to love someone who can't love you back," Aurora said, looking up at the older woman. "But I'm the one who can't love back properly. I can't love Tobias in the healthy, non-possessive way he deserves."

"No," Raven agreed sadly. "You can't. And recognizing that is perhaps the most loving thing you've ever done for him."

Aurora stared at the forest around them, seeing now why Raven had made the choice to stay away from her son. The most loving thing hadn't been attempted control or careful management of her dangerous impulses. It had been complete absence.

"If I go back," Aurora said slowly, "I'll fall into the same patterns. Maybe not immediately, maybe not obviously, but eventually. I'll start questioning his decisions again, guiding his choices, making myself essential to his wellbeing by undermining his confidence in his own judgment."

"Very likely," Raven agreed.

"And he doesn't owe me gratitude for saving his life all those years ago. He doesn't owe me central importance in his world." Aurora felt tears starting but didn't try to stop them. "A promise to dying parents doesn't justify a lifetime of control."

They sat in silence as the sun began to set, painting the mountainside in shades of gold and red. Aurora could feel her old life calling to her: Tobias, the school, the students who needed guidance, the community that looked to her for leadership. But she could also see, with devastating clarity, what her return would cost them all.

"The most protective thing I can do," Aurora said finally, "is protect him from me."

Raven reached over and squeezed Aurora's shoulder gently. "Now you understand what it means to love someone more than you love yourself."

As darkness fell and they made their way back to the shelter, Aurora felt something she'd never experienced before: the quiet strength that came from choosing someone else's wellbeing over her own emotional needs. It hurt more than any physical pain she'd ever endured, but it also felt clean in a way that all her previous choices never had.

"What will you do?" Raven asked as they settled by the fire.

Aurora looked around the simple shelter that had become her sanctuary, then out at the forest where her healing work was allowing new life to flourish. "I'll stay," she said quietly. "I'll learn to live without being needed. I'll find purpose in healing damaged places rather than controlling people."

"And when Tobias comes looking for you? Because he will."

Aurora's heart clenched at the thought, but her resolve held firm. "Then I'll be gone before he arrives. I'll become someone worthy of the trust his parents placed in me by never using it again."

Raven smiled with something that looked like pride mixed with infinite sadness. "You've learned the hardest lesson of all, Aurora. True love sometimes requires complete sacrifice."

CHAPTER TWENTY-ONE:
The Trap

The coffee cup slipped from Tobias's suddenly nerveless fingers, hitting the carpet with a dull thud. His heart hammered against his ribs as his mind raced through the implications. How had they found them? Were they being watched? Had their mission been compromised from the start?

Tobias's first instinct was to grab their bags and run. Find another flight, another route, anything to avoid this confrontation. But then his recent experience kicked in, weeks of successfully managing crises, of making hard decisions under pressure, of proving he could lead when leadership was required.

He was done running from problems. Time to face them head-on.

"Stay close," Tobias said quietly to Odion, standing up with deliberate calm. "But let me handle this."

They walked across the departure lounge with careful casualness, Tobias forcing himself to project confidence he didn't entirely feel. The advantage was his; last time he saw the couple, he'd proven he could defeat them both at the same time in direct magical combat. The problem was that they were in public, trying to be inconspicuous. Surrounded by innocent people, security cameras, and federal agents who wouldn't appreciate unexplained magical phenomena.

"Sabrina. Lucien." Tobias settled into an empty chair across from them, his tone pleasant and conversational. "What a coincidence."

Sabrina looked up from her magazine and smiled with what appeared to be genuine pleasure. She did not seem surprised at all to see him.

"Tobias! How lovely to see you. And Odion, of course." Her voice carried the warm professionalism of a teacher greeting former colleagues at a conference. "I had no idea you were traveling today."

"Educational research," Tobias replied smoothly. "Korean historical sites. You know how it is, always looking for new curriculum materials."

"How fascinating," Lucien chimed in, setting aside his own magazine. "Korean history is such a rich field. So many... undiscovered treasures to explore."

The words sounded innocent enough, but Tobias caught the subtle emphasis. They knew. Somehow, they knew exactly where his team was going and why.

Hunter appeared beside their small group, moving with the predatory grace that had once made him such an effective Rebellion operative. He nodded politely to Sabrina and Lucien without a hint of warmth.

"Lady. Gentleman." His tone suggested he was greeting strangers at a bus stop rather than people he'd once considered allies. "Excuse me, but I think they're about to start boarding."

Sabrina's smile faltered slightly at Hunter's complete indifference. Clearly, she'd expected some reaction: guilt, anger, defensive explanation. Instead, Hunter treated them like furniture, barely worth acknowledging.

"Hunter," she said, her voice taking on a note of false concern. "I hope you've been well. We were so worried when you... disappeared."

"Were you?" Hunter's tone remained politely disinterested. "That's nice."

Marina joined them as the gate agent announced pre-boarding for first class passengers. She immediately sensed the tension radiating from the group, her eyes darting between faces as she tried to assess the situation.

"Marina!" Sabrina's voice brightened with what sounded like genuine pleasure, not the fake joy she had been using with Tobias and Hunter. "How wonderful to see you again, dear. New colleagues already? That was fast."

She paused, exchanging a meaningful glance with Lucien before continuing with apparent concern.

"Didn't you just leave your previous group after being removed for... what was it, Lucien? Inappropriate behavior with a superior?"

Marina's face went white with shock and anger. "That's completely—I never—that's not what happened at all!"

"Of course not, dear," Sabrina said soothingly. "I'm sure there were... extenuating circumstances. There always are in these situations."

Lucien leaned forward with the expression of someone sharing helpful information. "Such a small world, isn't it? Especially in our educational circles. Marina's grandmother and I went to the same university, you know. Lovely woman. So accomplished with her... research methodologies."

Research methodologies? What did that mean? And why was this the first he was hearing about Marina's family connections?

"Thank you, Marina," Sabrina continued, her voice warm with gratitude, "for developing that tracking system to help us locate Aurora. For her own protection, of course. We're so concerned about her wellbeing."

"I didn't—" Marina started, then stopped, her voice rising with frustrated denial. "I'm not sharing anything with you! That's completely false!"

"That's complete bullshit and you know it," Hunter said flatly, his indifferent mask slipping for the first time. "Marina's been working with us for weeks. She saved Odion's life."

"She literally did save my life," Odion added, his analytical mind immediately spotting the logical flaws in their narrative. "I think I'd know if she was working against us."

But even as his team defended Marina, Tobias found Sabrina and Lucien's words echoing in his mind. The tracking system had been remarkably effective. Marina's skills had aligned perfectly with their needs. Her appearance in their group had been almost... convenient.

"Of course she saved you," Lucien said reasonably. "That's exactly what someone in her position would do. Build trust, prove indispensable, gain access to sensitive information. Standard intelligence gathering."

"You're wrong," Marina said, but her voice carried a note of desperation that made Tobias's suspicion deepen. If she had nothing to hide, why did she sound so defensive?

The gate agent announced general boarding, and passengers began forming lines with the practiced efficiency of experienced travelers. Around them, normal people worried about normal things like overhead bin space, seat assignments, and whether they'd packed enough clothes for their vacation. Tobias wished, just for a second, he could have his biggest worry be whether he packed swimwear.

"Well," Sabrina said, gathering her purse with graceful finality, "we should let you get to your... research. Such important work you're doing."

She stood, smoothing her dress, then turned back with what appeared to be genuine concern.

"Do take care of each other. Trust is such a fragile thing, especially when you're so far from home."

"Especially," Lucien added, shouldering his carry-on bag, "when so much depends on accurate information. And reliable sources."

They walked away toward the boarding line for the same Seoul flight, leaving his team standing in the departure lounge like survivors of a psychological bombing.

"Boarding Group A," the gate agent announced cheerfully.

Tobias fumbled for his boarding pass, his mind reeling. How had Marina known exactly where to find Aurora's trail? Why had she appeared just when they needed her specific water-tracking abilities? Her skills had been almost too perfect, her knowledge too comprehensive, her timing too convenient.

As they moved through the boarding process, Tobias found himself making a decision that felt like prudent leadership but tasted like paranoia. When they reached their row, he gestured Marina toward the window seat.

"You'll have a better view," he said pleasantly, settling into the middle seat beside her.

Behind them, Hunter and Odion took their assigned seats together, comfortable and trusting in each other's company. The contrast wasn't lost on Marina, who glanced between the seating arrangements with growing understanding.

"Tobias," she said quietly as the plane filled with passengers, "you know what they said isn't true, right?"

"Of course," Tobias replied, though he found himself cataloging her every movement. "Just trying to make sure everyone's comfortable for the long flight."

Marina's expression suggested she wasn't buying his explanation, but she didn't push the issue. Instead, she pulled out a book and settled into reading, though Tobias noticed she kept glancing at him from the corner of her eye.

Three hours into the flight

The plane had settled into the steady hum of long-distance travel, that peculiar suspension between departure and arrival where time seemed to move differently. Most passengers had pulled out books, tablets, or settled in for the first of what would likely be several naps during the fourteen-hour journey to Seoul.

Tobias found himself hyper-aware of every sound Marina made. The soft rustle of pages turning. The quiet sip of her drink. The way she shifted in her seat to get more comfortable. Each movement felt loaded with potential significance, though he couldn't articulate what he was looking for.

Behind them, he could hear Hunter and Odion's conversation growing more animated. The flight attendant had just finished drink service, and both men had opted for alcohol with their meal; a decision that seemed to be loosening their tongues considerably.

"I'm just saying," Hunter was explaining with the patient tone of someone making an obviously correct point, "you could've warned me that you teleporting was going to be like being turned inside out by a blender operated by someone having a seizure."

"I could've warned you?!" Odion protested, his voice slightly louder than it had been an hour ago. "You could've SAID teleportation would be dangerous! You're the one with experience!"

"Odion, I know for a fact that Tobias drilled it into your head about five thousand times before you teleported the first time that this would be dangerous. Especially after the two of you teleported out of Rebellion headquarters? You really didn't pick up on that?"

"Tobias said it would be 'challenging,'" Odion replied with the careful enunciation of someone who'd had just enough wine to be honest. "He said it would require 'significant energy and focus.' He did not say it would feel like my soul was being pureed."

Marina glanced back at them with amusement, and Tobias noticed she was following their conversation with genuine interest rather than the polite tolerance he might have expected.

"You know," Hunter continued, "back when I was working with the Rebellion, we had protocols for this stuff. Safety briefings, preparation techniques, aftercare procedures—"

"Aftercare procedures?" Odion interrupted, sounding fascinated. "For teleportation?"

"Oh yeah. Crackers, ginger ale, sometimes a little magical energy boost if someone was really struggling. Ted used to keep these special motion sickness bags that were enchanted to neutralize any... unfortunate side effects."

"Please tell me you're making this up," Odion said, but he was laughing.

"I am absolutely not making this up. Marina, back me up here. The Rebellion had protocols for everything, right?"

Marina turned around in her seat with a slight smile. "We had a thirty-seven-page manual on proper teleportation etiquette," she confirmed. "Color-coded charts for different distances, recommended pre-jump meals, even guidelines for appropriate conversation topics during group jumps."

"Appropriate conversation topics?" Tobias found himself asking despite his suspicions. "Like maybe…not discussing teleportation on a crowded airplane?"

"Oh, no one's listening to us, Toby!" Hunter exclaimed, and he was right; all the surrounding passengers were much too preoccupied with their television shows, movies, books, or naps to pay them any attention.

"Nothing controversial," Marina continued like she hadn't been interrupted. "Weather was always safe. Current events were discouraged because they might trigger emotional responses that could destabilize the teleportation. Sports were okay unless anyone had strong team loyalties."

"One time," Hunter added, grinning at the memory, "this guy Marcus got into an argument about baseball statistics mid-jump. We ended up materializing in a Wendy's parking lot instead of our cruise ship warehouse." Hunter shook his head, smirking. "Luckily, Marcus didn't end up draining the Wendy's of all the frosties like you did, Odion."

"That cannot be true," Odion said, wiping tears from his eyes.

"Scout's honor," Hunter replied solemnly. "Though to be fair, I was never actually a scout. Got kicked out of the meeting when I was eight for asking too many questions about the knot-tying demonstrations."

"What kind of questions could possibly get you kicked out of Scouts?" Marina asked.

"Well, apparently asking whether the slip knot could be used for anything 'more permanent' than securing camping equipment was considered 'inappropriate for the age group.'"

Odion was laughing so hard he was starting to wheeze. "You asked about—oh my god, you were eight years old!"

"I was a very practical child," Hunter said defensively. "If you're going to teach a skill, you should cover all the applications."

Even Tobias found himself fighting a smile. Whatever else Hunter might be, he was genuinely funny when he relaxed enough to let his guard down.

Six hours into the flight

The wine had definitely been a good decision, Odion reflected as he settled back in his seat with his second small bottle. The cramped quarters and endless hours seemed much more manageable when viewed through a slight alcoholic haze, and Hunter had turned out to be surprisingly good company.

AURORA

"No, no, you're not understanding the severity of the situation," Hunter was explaining in a stage whisper that was probably audible three rows away. "Miss Rosa took her gardening very seriously. When I accidentally stepped on her prized tomato plant, she made me write a formal apology letter. To the plant."

"To the plant itself?" Odion whispered back, clearly delighted.

"One full page, handwritten, explaining why I was sorry and promising to be more careful in the future. She made me read it aloud to the entire garden."

"Did you actually do it?"

"Of course I did it. You didn't cross Miss Rosa. She once lectured a delivery truck driver for fifteen minutes because he parked too close to her roses, and they might have felt 'vehicular anxiety.'"

"Vehicular anxiety," Odion repeated slowly, grinning. "That's...that's actually kind of beautiful."

"She was convinced that plants had feelings more complex than most people's. Used to talk to them like they were her grandchildren. 'How are you feeling today, little ones? Do you need more water? Are you getting enough sunlight for your delicate constitutions?'"

Tobias could hear the genuine affection in Hunter's voice as he talked about this woman from his childhood. It was hard to reconcile this gentle nostalgia with the man who had burned down Jefferson High School.

"She sounds wonderful," Odion said softly.

"She was. When my parents kicked me out for being gay, Miss Rosa was the one who made sure I had food. She'd invite me over for dinner at least three times a week, always with some excuse like needing help with her garden or wanting someone to watch her soap operas with."

Hunter paused, and when he continued, his voice was quieter.

"I never told her I was gay, you know. Never had to. She just... knew. And she never made it a thing. Never asked questions or gave advice. Just made sure I knew her door was always open."

"That's the kind of love that saves people," Odion said, and Tobias could hear real understanding in his voice.

"Yeah. It really is." Hunter was quiet for a moment, then asked, "What about you? I mean, I know we don't really know each other that well, but...did you have someone like that? Someone who just accepted you completely?"

Odion was swirling the wine in his small plastic cup. "You know what's funny? I think I'm finding that now. Here, with this group. With Tobias and everyone at Bellwater."

"Found family," Hunter said, understanding immediately.

"Exactly. I mean, I had family growing up, but..." Odion trailed off, then seemed to shake himself. "But it's different when you choose each other, you know? When someone looks at you and decides you're worth keeping around, not because they have to, but because they want to."

"That's what Miss Rosa was for me," Hunter agreed. "And honestly? That's what Tobias was too, for a long time. The first person who ever really saw me and didn't try to change me."

"Even when you were being an absolute nightmare?" Odion asked with a slight grin.

Hunter laughed. "Especially when I was being an absolute nightmare. God, the patience that man has. I put him through hell for years, and he just... kept trying to reach me."

"Is that what the kidnapping was about?" Odion asked gently. "Trying to protect that relationship?"

The question hung in the air between them. Hunter took a long sip of his wine before answering.

"Yeah," he said finally. "Yeah, that's exactly what it was about. I was so terrified of losing the one person who'd ever really loved me that I...well, I nearly destroyed him trying to keep him safe."

"I get it," Odion said quietly. "Not the kidnapping part, obviously, but the fear. When you've never had a real family before, when you finally find people who accept you completely...the thought of losing that is terrifying."

"Exactly." Hunter met Odion's eyes with something like relief. "I don't think I've ever had anyone understand that before."

"Well, you've got people who understand it now," Odion said. "All of us. We're all here because Tobias saw something worth saving in us. We're all part of this weird little family he's built."

"Even Marina?" Hunter asked, glancing toward the front of the plane.

"Especially Marina," Odion said firmly. "She's been through hell, and she's still here trying to help. That takes real strength."

Tobias felt something uncomfortable twist in his stomach at Odion's words. Here were two people who had found genuine understanding in each other, building the kind of trust and acceptance that made a team into a family. And what was he doing? Watching Marina for signs of betrayal, cataloging her every movement for evidence of deception.

Nine hours into the flight

The cabin lights had dimmed for the overnight portion of the journey, creating an intimate atmosphere that made quiet conversations feel even more personal. Most passengers were attempting to sleep, though with limited success given the uncomfortable angles required by economy seating.

Behind him, Hunter and Odion had moved on to comparing their most embarrassing teaching moments, their voices now carrying the easy familiarity of people who'd discovered they genuinely liked each other. Tobias rather thought they perhaps had had a tiny bit too much to drink, but. They were grown men on a fourteen hour flight. Who was he to judge?

"So there I am," Odion was saying quietly, "trying to explain algebraic equations to a room full of sixteen-year-olds who clearly think math is a form of medieval torture, when this kid—let's call him Brandon because that was his name and he deserves to be remembered for this—raises his hand."

"Oh no," Hunter murmured with the sympathy of a fellow educator.

"Brandon says, and I quote, 'Mr. Montgomery, when are we ever going to use this in real life?' Classic question, right? Every math teacher's heard it a thousand times."

"What did you tell him?"

"Well, I started into my prepared response about problem-solving skills and logical thinking, but then Brandon interrupts me—interrupts me!—and says, 'Because my dad says math is stupid and he makes more money than you do.'"

Hunter sucked in a breath. "Ouch."

"Twenty-eight other students immediately turn to look at me, waiting to see how I'm going to handle this public challenge to my authority and life choices."

"What did you do?"

"I panicked," Odion admitted cheerfully. "Completely panicked. So I said the first thing that came into my head, which was, 'Well, Brandon, your dad also thought it was a good idea to name you Brandon, so perhaps his judgment isn't as reliable as you think.'"

Hunter made a choking sound. "You said that to a student?"

"In front of the entire class. The room went dead silent for about ten seconds, and then this girl named Sarah, the same girl that Brandon had a crush on, mind you, started laughing. Then everyone was laughing. Brandon turned bright red and slumped down in his seat."

"Oh my god, you destroyed a child's soul in front of his peers."

"I felt terrible immediately," Odion continued. "Like, genuinely awful. So I spent the rest of the class period explaining how names are cultural artifacts that reflect family history and personal meaning, and that there's nothing inherently wrong with any name, including Brandon, which actually has quite noble etymological roots."

"Did that help?"

"Brandon spent the rest of the semester working harder in my class than any other student. Got a B+ on his final exam."

"So your teaching method is to psychologically devastate students and then rebuild their self-esteem through etymology lessons?"

"It's a very specialized approach," Odion said with dignity. "I don't recommend it for everyone."

"At least you didn't strangle Brandon with a sunflower like Aurora would've done."

Tobias grimaced at this comment, not entirely surprised that Hunter said it but still not thrilled about it. He did, however, find himself…not caring so much about the comment at this point.

"I hadn't thought of it that way, but… yeah, maybe. What about you? Please tell me you have an equally horrifying story of pedagogical failure."

"Oh, do I ever. Picture this: my second day teaching high school chemistry. I'm trying to demonstrate a simple reaction, just mixing baking soda and vinegar, totally harmless stuff."

"Why do I feel like this isn't going to end with a gentle fizzing sound?"

"Because you've clearly met me. So I'm explaining the chemical reaction, writing the equation on the board, really trying to be the engaging, enthusiastic teacher who makes science come alive."

"And?"

"And I may have... slightly miscalculated the proportions."

"How slightly?"

"Well, let's just say that when you use an entire box of baking soda and a full bottle of vinegar in a closed container, the reaction is somewhat more vigorous than expected."

"Hunter. No."

"The container exploded. Baking soda paste hit the ceiling. Vinegar sprayed everywhere. I had one kid dive under his desk like we were under artillery fire."

Odion was shaking with silent laughter. "Please tell me no one was hurt."

"Everyone was fine, but the classroom smelled like salad dressing for a week. And the principal made me attend a mandatory seminar on 'Laboratory Safety Protocols' that was clearly designed for people who had no business being near anything more dangerous than a crayon."

"Did you at least learn from this experience?"

"Oh, absolutely. I learned that if you're going to accidentally create a chemical explosion in front of teenagers, you'd better own it completely. So when the smoke cleared, I just looked at the class and said, 'And that, my friends, is why we start with small quantities when experimenting with unknown reactions.'"

AURORA

"You pretended it was intentional?"

"Not only did I pretend it was intentional, I made them all write up lab reports analyzing what had gone wrong and how to prevent it in the future. Turned my complete failure into a teachable moment."

"That's actually... kind of genius."

"The kids loved it. Word got around that Mr. Diaz's chemistry class was where stuff actually exploded, and suddenly I had students begging to transfer into my sections."

"So your teaching method is controlled demolition?"

"When necessary, yes."

Marina shifted in her seat beside Tobias, stretching as much as the cramped space allowed. She'd been awake for most of their conversation, occasionally smiling at particularly funny moments, but mostly just listening with the patient attention of someone enduring a very long journey.

"They're really hitting it off," she said quietly to Tobias. "It's nice to see Hunter relaxed like this. He's been so tense since we started traveling together."

Tobias nodded, though her comment only added to his growing unease. How much attention had Marina been paying to Hunter's emotional state? Was she monitoring all of them, cataloging their reactions and relationships for some larger purpose?

Eleven hours into the flight

The moment that changed everything happened while Marina was fully awake and alert.

Tobias was returning from the bathroom, navigating the narrow aisle with the careful steps of someone whose legs had gone numb from sitting too long. Marina was reading her book, occasionally glancing up at the other passengers with the mild interest of someone people-watching to pass time. Hunter and Odion had finally settled into quieter conversation, their earlier wine-fueled hilarity having mellowed into genuine friendship.

As Tobias approached his row, Sabrina emerged from the first-class cabin, moving toward the bathrooms at the back of the plane. She walked with her usual graceful confidence, acknowledging other passengers with polite nods and small smiles.

When she reached Tobias's row, she paused.

"Excuse me," she said quietly, gesturing for him to step aside so she could pass.

Tobias pressed himself against the armrest of an empty seat, giving her room in the narrow aisle. As she moved past him, Sabrina's gaze fell on Marina, who looked up from her book with polite acknowledgment.

And Sabrina winked.

Not at Tobias. Not at the air in general. A deliberate, unmistakable wink directed specifically at Marina, accompanied by the slightest curve of her lips.

Marina's reaction was... nothing. She simply returned Sabrina's gaze with neutral politeness, the way she might acknowledge any passing stranger, then returned to her book as if the interaction had never happened.

But Tobias saw it all. The wink, Marina's complete lack of response, the casual way Sabrina continued toward the bathroom as if she'd done nothing more significant than stretch her legs.

The gesture lasted maybe half a second. But to Tobias, it felt like watching his worst fears confirmed in slow motion.

As Sabrina disappeared into the bathroom, Tobias settled back into his seat, his heart hammering against his ribs.

"Good book?" he asked Marina, his voice coming out rougher than he'd intended.

Marina looked up from the pages. "It's interesting. It's about the Korean War. Figured I should learn something about where we're going."

"Smart thinking," Tobias managed.

She studied his expression with growing concern. "Are you okay? You look like you've seen a ghost."

Tobias stared at her, searching her face for any sign of... what? Guilt? Recognition? Some indication that she'd been aware of Sabrina's gesture and chosen to ignore it for his benefit?

"I'm fine," he said, though he was anything but fine.

His mind raced through possibilities, each one worse than the last. Had Marina been expecting that wink? Was she somehow communicating with Sabrina without his knowledge? Was her calm reaction evidence of innocence or proof of training?

The more he thought about it, the more sinister every detail became. Marina's convenient appearance in their group. Her almost too-perfect tracking abilities. Her willingness to help after everything Aurora had done to her. Her casual knowledge of Rebellion protocols. Even her choice of reading material—was she really learning about Korean history, or was she preparing for a mission she already knew the details of?

"Tobias," Marina said gently, "you're staring at me again. Are you sure you're okay?"

He forced himself to look away, to appear normal. "Just tired. Long flight."

But inside, his thoughts were spinning out of control. How much had Marina shared with the Rebellion? Did they know about Aurora's exact location? Were Sabrina and Lucien planning to reach her first?

Worse still: was this entire mission a trap?

Twelve and a half hours into the flight

Tobias couldn't take it anymore. The paranoid thoughts had been building for over an hour, each innocent action from Marina taking on sinister significance in his mind. When she excused herself to the bathroom, he immediately turned around in his seat to face Hunter and Odion.

Both men looked up from their conversation with mild surprise, the easy camaraderie of the past several hours evident in their relaxed postures.

"We need to talk," Tobias said quietly. "Now."

Hunter glanced around the dimly lit cabin, most passengers still attempting to sleep. "Here?"

"Yes, here. I need to ask you both something, and I need honest answers."

Odion leaned forward, his expression growing serious despite the wine still in his system. "What's wrong?"

Tobias took a deep breath, trying to organize his thoughts. "How well do we really know Marina?"

Hunter and Odion exchanged a glance, clearly not understanding where this was coming from.

"What do you mean?" Hunter asked carefully.

"I mean, think about it logically. She appears in our group right when we need someone with water-tracking abilities. Her skills are exactly what we need to find Aurora. Her timing was perfect, almost too perfect."

"Tobias," Odion said gently, though his words were slightly slurred from the wine, "she saved my life. I was literally dying, and she knew exactly what to do."

"Which could be seen as building trust," Tobias pressed. "Making herself indispensable to the team."

Hunter's expression was growing concerned, but not for the reasons Tobias expected. "Toby, what brought this on? Has something happened?"

Tobias glanced toward the bathroom, making sure Marina was still out of earshot. "Sabrina winked at her," he said quietly. "While Marina was sitting right there, awake and reading, Sabrina walked past our seats and winked directly at her."

The silence that followed was deafening.

"You're sure?" Odion asked finally, his analytical mind cutting through the alcohol haze.

"I'm positive. It was deliberate, specific. Like they were communicating somehow."

Hunter rubbed his face with both hands, looking exhausted. "Toby, that could mean anything. Maybe Sabrina was just being weird. Maybe she was trying to mess with your head, which seems to be working perfectly. Maybe she's drunk and was trying to hit on Marina, I've always thought she could do better than Lucien--"

"Or maybe Marina has been working with them all along," Tobias shot back. "Maybe this entire search has been orchestrated to lead us exactly where they want us to go."

"That's..." Odion started, then stopped, his expression growing more serious. "Actually, that's not entirely impossible."

Hunter shot him a sharp look. "Don't encourage this."

"I'm not encouraging anything," Odion said defensively. "I'm just saying that we should consider all possibilities. Marina did show up at exactly the right time with exactly the right skills."

Tobias felt vindicated by Odion's agreement, but Hunter looked increasingly frustrated.

"This is insane," Hunter said quietly. "Marina hasn't done anything suspicious. She's been helpful, honest, and she literally saved Odion's life. Now you want to suspect her because Sabrina made a face?"

"It wasn't just a face," Tobias insisted. "It was deliberate communication."

"Or it was Sabrina trying to make you paranoid about the one person who's been genuinely helpful," Hunter countered. "Which, again, seems to be working perfectly."

"But what if Tobias is right?" Odion asked, his voice taking on the careful precision he used when working through a complex problem. "What if Marina has been feeding them information? What if they know exactly where we're going?"

"Then we deal with that when we get there," Hunter said firmly. "But I'm not going to start treating our allies like enemies based on a facial expression."

Tobias felt something snap inside him. "Our allies? Hunter, you of all people should understand that allies can become enemies. You did it yourself."

The words hung in the air like a slap. Hunter's expression went cold, all the warmth and openness from their earlier conversation evaporating.

"That was different," Hunter said quietly.

"Was it? You were working with the Rebellion. You were trusted. You had access to information. And then you switched sides when it suited you."

"I switched sides because they ordered me to murder my best friend," Hunter said, his voice tight with anger. "That's hardly the same thing as Marina helping us track down Aurora."

AURORA

Odion held up a hand before the argument could escalate further. "Look, we can argue about Marina's motivations all we want, but the fact is, we're committed to this mission now. We're on a plane to Seoul, we have a plan to find Aurora, and whether Marina is trustworthy or not, we need to see this through."

"But we need to be careful," Tobias pressed. "We need to watch her, make sure she's not compromising our mission."

"Watch her how?" Hunter asked. "By treating her like a prisoner? By questioning her every move? By destroying whatever trust we've built?"

Before Tobias could respond, he saw Marina returning from the bathroom. He quickly turned back around in his seat, his heart pounding.

As Marina settled back into her seat, she immediately noticed the tension radiating from his posture.

"Everything okay?" she asked.

"Fine," Tobias said, though nothing felt fine anymore.

Behind him, he could hear Hunter and Odion's conversation resume, but it was quieter now, more subdued. The easy camaraderie of earlier had been replaced by something heavier.

CHAPTER TWENTY-TWO:
Poor Decisions

The customs line at Incheon International Airport moved with the efficient slowness of international bureaucracy. Tobias stood behind a family of German tourists, watching the uniformed officials process passports with methodical precision. His body ached from the fourteen-hour flight, his eyes felt like they'd been rubbed with sandpaper, and every muscle in his back had apparently decided to stage a revolt against airplane seating.

But none of that mattered. Aurora was out there, probably dying, and every minute they spent on paperwork and procedures was another minute she suffered alone.

"Next," the customs official called in accented English.

Tobias stepped forward and handed over his passport, forcing his expression into the bland pleasantness of a tourist. "Educational research," he said when asked about his visit, the same line they'd rehearsed. "Korean historical sites."

The stamp came down with official finality, and Tobias was through. He waited in the arrivals area, watching his team emerge one by one from the customs maze. Hunter looked rumpled and irritated. Odion moved carefully, like someone fighting a wine hangover with limited success. Marina appeared last, her blue hair drawing curious glances from other travelers.

"Transportation?" Hunter asked as they regrouped near the exit.

"Rental car," Tobias replied, checking his phone for the confirmation email. "Should be waiting for us."

They collected their vehicle (a modest sedan that looked disappointingly normal for a car that would soon be crossing international borders) and piled in with their luggage. Tobias took the driver's seat, plugging coordinates into the GPS while the others settled into their seats.

"Hotel first?" Odion asked hopefully. "Maybe a shower and a few hours of sleep before we—"

"No," Tobias said firmly, starting the engine. "We go straight to the border. Every hour we delay gives Sabrina and Lucien more time to reach Aurora first."

Hunter turned in the passenger seat to stare at him. "Toby, we've been awake for over twenty hours. None of us are thinking clearly—"

"I'm thinking perfectly clearly," Tobias interrupted, pulling out of the parking structure with more aggression than was strictly necessary. "Aurora is dying somewhere in those mountains, and we're the only ones who can help her. A few hours of sleep isn't worth the risk that we'll be too late."

"But if we're exhausted when we find her—" Odion began.

"Then we deal with that when it happens." Tobias's voice carried the flat authority of someone who'd made up his mind. "We're going to the border. Now."

In the rearview mirror, he caught Hunter and Odion exchanging a look of concerned resignation. Marina sat quietly in her corner of the back seat, saying nothing. Her silence only added to Tobias's unease. Was she relieved they were moving quickly toward some predetermined rendezvous?

The drive north took three hours through increasingly rural landscape. Mountains rose on either side of the highway, and the signs became less frequent as they approached the border region. Tobias found himself checking the rearview mirror constantly, looking for cars that might be following them, though the paranoid part of his brain wondered if the real threat was already sitting in his back seat.

They stopped once for gas and supplies, stocking up on water, energy bars, and basic first aid materials. Marina bought a small Korean phrasebook, claiming it might be useful if they encountered civilians. To Tobias, even this seemed suspicious; was she really planning to communicate with locals, or did she already know exactly where they were going?

You're being paranoid, he told himself as they got back on the road. But the image of Sabrina's wink kept replaying in his mind, and Marina's calm competence felt increasingly unnatural.

Two hours later, they reached the border region.

Tobias parked the car behind a cluster of trees about half a mile from the official crossing point, where they could observe without being seen. Through binoculars, he could make out the guard posts, the razor wire, the serious-looking soldiers who took their jobs very seriously indeed.

"There," Marina said, pointing to a section of fence that looked slightly less fortified. "Hunter's contacts said that area has the most predictable patrol schedule. If we time it right—"

She stopped mid-sentence, her finger still pointing toward the fence. Tobias followed her gaze and felt his blood turn to ice.

Two familiar figures were approaching the main guard post. Sabrina Braithwaite in her elegant red dress, Lucien Rodson beside her in his rumpled khakis. They walked with casual confidence toward the heavily armed border guards.

"What the hell are they doing?" Hunter whispered.

"Getting themselves arrested," Odion replied grimly. "Or worse."

They watched in fascination and horror as Sabrina approached the lead guard, gesturing animatedly as though explaining something urgent. Even from this distance, they could see the guard's posture shift from routine alertness to high tension.

"She's warning them about something," Marina said quietly. "Look at their body language."

She was right. Within minutes, additional guards appeared. Radios crackled. The entire border crossing shifted to what looked like high alert status.

"They're warning them about us," Tobias said, his stomach sinking. "They're telling the guards to watch for American infiltrators or something."

"But why would they?" Odion asked, then stopped. "Unless they want to make sure we can't cross easily."

"Force us to take bigger risks," Hunter agreed. "Make us more vulnerable when we do get through."

They watched as Sabrina and Lucien finished their conversation with the guards and began walking back toward the road. But as the couple moved away from the guard post, something strange happened.

"Wait," Marina said, adjusting the binoculars. "Something's not right."

She was correct. As Sabrina and Lucien moved further from the guards, their images began to shimmer and fade, like heat mirages on hot asphalt. Within moments, they had completely disappeared.

"Apparitions," Hunter breathed. "Those weren't really them at all."

"Which means they're nearby," Tobias said grimly, "but not where we can see them."

The implications hit them all at once. Sabrina and Lucien were playing a much more sophisticated game than simple pursuit. They were actively sabotaging the mission from a safe distance, using magical deception to turn the border guards into unwitting allies.

"Son of a bitch," Tobias swore, lowering his binoculars. "Our original plan is completely shot."

The border crossing now bristled with heightened security. Guards who had been casually manning their posts were now alert and watchful. Additional patrols had been called up. Whatever Sabrina's apparition had told them, it had put the entire area on high alert.

"We could wait," Odion suggested hopefully. "Come back tomorrow when things have calmed down."

"No!" Tobias snapped. "We can't afford to wait. Who knows what other sabotage they're planning, or whether they'll reach Aurora first."

He studied the border fence through the binoculars, his mind racing through options. The increased security made stealth approach much more difficult, but not impossible. It would just require more risk.

"Do we try teleporting?"

"No."

Hunter's voice was surprisingly firm. Tobias looked up at him, and saw Hunter looking at Odion, who looked uncomfortable. Tobias had forgotten what happened the last time Odion had tried teleportation. Sighing, Tobias returned to his binoculars.

"We're going to have to split up," he decided. "Create a distraction to draw the guards away from the weakest section of fence."

"What kind of distraction?" Hunter asked, though his tone suggested he already suspected he wouldn't like the answer.

"Marina and I will approach the main crossing point," Tobias explained. "Act like lost tourists, ask for directions, keep their attention focused away from the fence. While they're dealing with us, you and Odion slip through at the weak point."

Hunter frowned. "Why not me and you for the distraction? I've got more experience with this kind of thing."

Tobias met his eyes steadily. "Because we've met, Hunter. You'll burn the gates down two seconds after trouble starts. The last thing we need is to start a war with North Korea."

Despite everything, Hunter snorted with amusement. "Fair point."

"But Tobias," Odion said, his face pale with more than just hangover, "what if something goes wrong? What if they separate us and we can't find each other again?"

"Then you and Hunter continue the mission," Tobias replied firmly. "Find Aurora. Help her. Don't worry about us."

They spent twenty minutes coordinating watches, establishing rendezvous points both for the border crossing and once inside North Korea, and reviewing Marina's tracking data. Hunter took it upon himself to scry parts of North Korea that were walkable from the main gate, as potential rendezvous points. They found one; a small clearing about a half a mile from the border that would be easily camouflaged if need be. There was no sign of Sabrina or Lucien, though. The plan was simple enough to work but dangerous enough to go catastrophically wrong. Exactly the kind of desperate scheme that exhausted people convinced themselves was brilliant.

"Ready?" Tobias asked Marina as they prepared to walk toward the border crossing.

She nodded, shouldering her small backpack. "Let's go be tourists."

They approached the guard post with the casual confidence of people who belonged there, Marina chattering about historical sites while Tobias nodded and pointed at landmarks. To any observer, they looked like exactly what they claimed to be: academic researchers who had gotten turned around and needed directions.

"Excuse me," Tobias called to the nearest guard in his carefully practiced Korean phrases. "We're looking for historical sites? Wartime memorials?"

The guard approached with the professional wariness of someone whose job was to be suspicious of everyone. His English was limited but functional.

"You cannot be here," he said firmly. "This is restricted area. You must go back."

"Oh, we're so sorry," Marina said, pulling out her tourist map with exaggerated confusion. "We thought the historical markers were this way. Could you show us the correct direction?"

As she spoke, she deliberately dropped her backpack, spilling tourist brochures and water bottles across the ground. Both guards immediately moved to help gather the scattered items, their attention completely focused on the harmless-seeming tourists.

Perfect.

Through his peripheral vision, Tobias could see Hunter and Odion moving through the trees toward the weak section of fence. They moved with careful stealth, taking advantage of the guards' distraction.

"You must go to visitor center," the second guard was explaining, pointing back toward the main road. "No tourists allowed in border zone."

"Of course, of course," Tobias said, helping Marina collect her scattered belongings. "We just got turned around. These mountain roads all look the same to us."

The distraction was working perfectly. Both guards were now completely engaged with directing the lost tourists, their backs turned to the fence where Hunter and Odion were making their crossing.

But then one of the guards' radios crackled to life.

AURORA

Rapid Korean burst from the speaker, and Tobias caught enough words to understand the gist: movement detected, possible infiltrators, all units to high alert.

The guard's demeanor changed instantly. His hand moved to his weapon as he barked orders to his companion. Within seconds, additional guards were jogging toward their position from other parts of the crossing.

"Time to go," Marina said quietly, reading the situation with the same clarity Tobias felt.

They started backing away from the increasingly agitated guards, hands raised in universal gestures of peaceful surrender. But the guards weren't interested in peaceful anymore. Shouts echoed across the border zone as more soldiers appeared.

"Run," Tobias said.

They ran.

Gunshots cracked behind them as they sprinted toward the tree line, bullets whining through the air with deadly intent. Tobias zigzagged through the underbrush, his heart hammering against his ribs as branches tore at his clothes.

He was so focused on reaching cover that he didn't see the guard who had flanked them until it was almost too late. The muzzle flash lit up the forest, and Tobias felt something hot and sharp tear past his face, missing him by inches.

Then Marina slammed into him, her shoulder catching him in the chest with enough force to send them both tumbling to the ground. They rolled behind a fallen log just as another volley of shots splintered the bark above their heads.

"Are you hit?" Tobias gasped, checking himself for wounds.

"My arm," Marina said through gritted teeth, clutching her left shoulder. Blood was seeping between her fingers where the bullet had scraped along her upper arm.

Tobias felt something cold and sharp twist in his chest as he saw the blood. She'd saved his life. Taken a bullet meant for him without hesitation.

"I'm sorry," he said quickly, pulling his shirt off to use as a makeshift bandage. "I'm sorry I doubted you. I should never have—"

"Later," Marina interrupted, pressing the cloth against her wound. "Right now we need to get out of here."

More shouts echoed through the forest as the guards organized a search. They had seconds before being surrounded.

"Can you teleport us?" Marina asked.

Tobias nodded, though his magical energy felt depleted from stress and exhaustion. "Hold on to me."

Marina grabbed his arm with her good hand, and Tobias reached deep for the power he needed. The world dissolved around them in a rush of disorienting magic, and they rematerialized half a mile away in a small clearing. Past the border, into North Korea.

Both of them collapsed immediately, breathing hard from the adrenaline and magical exertion.

"Did they make it?" Marina asked, checking her wounded arm.

Tobias closed his eyes and tried to sense Hunter and Odion through their magical connection. For a terrifying moment, he felt nothing. Then, faintly, he caught the familiar warmth of their presence.

"They're alive," he said with relief. "Across the border."

"Good." Marina winced as she adjusted the makeshift bandage. "Because this is going to hurt for a while."

Tobias looked at her, really looked at her, for the first time since

Sabrina's mind games on the airplane. Marina's blue hair was matted with sweat and dirt. Her face was pale with pain and exhaustion. Blood stained her shirt where she'd taken a bullet to protect him.

She looked like exactly what she was: someone who'd risked everything to help people she barely knew, because it was the right thing to do.

"Thank you," he said quietly. "For saving my life. And I'm sorry for... for being suspicious. Sabrina got in my head, and I let paranoia poison my judgment."

Marina managed a weak smile. "Well, now we're even. You saved me from Aurora's basement. I saved you from North Korean bullets. That's what teammates do."

Teammates. The word hit Tobias with surprising warmth. Not allies of convenience or reluctant partners, but actual teammates who looked out for each other.

"Can you travel?" he asked, helping her to her feet.

"I can manage," Marina said, though she leaned on him more than she probably wanted to admit. "Where to now?"

Tobias pulled out Marina's tracking equipment, checking their position against her carefully mapped coordinates. "Now we wait for Hunter and Odion," he said carefully. "Once they meet us here, we can proceed as planned."

They settled into the small clearing Hunter had identified during his scrying, using fallen logs as makeshift seats while Marina tended to her wound with supplies from her backpack. The forest around them was eerily quiet, the kind of silence that made every snapping twig sound like approaching footsteps.

"How's the arm?" Tobias asked, watching Marina work with practiced efficiency.

"It'll be fine," she replied, cleaning the bullet graze with antiseptic that made her wince. "Just a flesh wound, really. I've had worse."

Tobias found himself wondering what kind of life led to casual comments about having worse injuries than bullet wounds, but he didn't ask. Everyone in their strange little family had scars they didn't talk about.

After what felt like hours but was probably only thirty minutes, they heard the soft crunch of footsteps approaching through the underbrush. Both Tobias and Marina tensed, ready to run or fight, until Hunter's familiar voice called out quietly.

"Please tell me you're not pointing weapons at us."

"Hunter!" Tobias jumped up, relief flooding through him as Hunter and Odion emerged from the trees. Both men looked exhausted and disheveled, their clothes torn from branches and their faces streaked with dirt, but they were moving under their own power and didn't appear to be bleeding.

"Thank God you made it," Odion said, his voice thick with genuine emotion. "When we heard all those gunshots—"

"Are you hurt?" Hunter interrupted, his eyes immediately finding Marina's makeshift bandage.

"I'm fine," Marina said quickly. "What about you two? Any trouble crossing?"

"Actually, no," Odion said, settling onto one of the fallen logs with obvious relief. "Your distraction worked perfectly. All the guards went chasing after the gunshots, left the weak section of fence completely unmonitored."

"We slipped through while they were all focused on you," Hunter added. "Probably the easiest border crossing I've ever made, which is saying something."

Tobias felt something tight in his chest finally loosen. They were all here. All alive. All together in a foreign country where they definitely shouldn't be, but together nonetheless.

Without really thinking about it, he stepped forward and pulled both Hunter and Odion into a fierce bear hug. The relief, gratitude, and genuine affection he felt for these two men who'd risked everything to help him save Aurora flowed through the connection, and he felt their own magical energy respond and strengthen in return. When they broke apart after several seconds, all three of them looked visibly refreshed despite the circumstances.

"Marina," Tobias said, turning toward her with an invitation in his voice and his outstretched arms.

She looked up from where she was applying a proper bandage to her arm and shook her head with a gentle smile. "Thanks, but I'm good. Physical contact isn't really my thing for healing."

Tobias lowered his arms, feeling slightly awkward but not wanting to press. "Oh. Is there anything we can do to help?"

"I've got it covered," Marina said, pulling a small vial of what looked like herbal tincture from her first aid supplies. She took a careful sip, then applied a few drops directly to her wound. Almost immediately, her color improved and the tension around her eyes eased. "My grandmother's recipe. Works better for me than hugs ever did."

"Different people feel loved in different ways," Hunter said matter-of-factly, settling beside Odion on their makeshift log bench. "Physical touch is just one option. Some people prefer acts of service, quality time, words of affirmation, gifts..." He trailed off with a slight shrug. "What matters is figuring out what actually works for each person."

Tobias nodded, filing this information away for future reference. The magic system he'd learned at Bellwater had always emphasized physical affection as the primary way to restore magical energy, but it made sense that it wouldn't work for everyone. People were too complex to all respond to exactly the same thing.

As the four of them settled into the clearing, Tobias found himself really looking at his team for the first time since they'd left Seoul. All of them were running on fumes. Odion was fighting off what was probably still a minor hangover on top of exhaustion from the border crossing. Hunter looked like he'd been awake for days, which he basically had. Marina was injured and clearly in more pain than she was admitting. And Tobias himself felt like he'd been run over by a truck.

"We need to stop," he said suddenly.

The others looked at him with varying degrees of confusion.

"Stop what?" Hunter asked.

"This. All of this. The rushing, the pushing forward on no sleep, the making critical decisions when we're all running on adrenaline and bad judgment." Tobias gestured around the clearing. "We need to eat something substantial, get cleaned up, and sleep for a few hours before we continue."

"And Aurora?" Odion asked.

"Will still be there in eight hours," Tobias interrupted firmly. "And we'll be in much better shape to actually help her if we're not stumbling around the wilderness half-dead from exhaustion."

He looked around at their faces, seeing the resistance he'd expected but also relief that someone had finally said what they were all thinking.

"We're in hostile territory," he continued, his voice taking on the authoritative tone he'd been learning to use as a leader. "If we accidentally run into a patrol because we're too tired to be careful, we'll be worse than useless to Aurora. And if we do find her, she's going to need us at full strength, not…whatever this is."

Tobias gestured to their bedraggled group with a rueful smile. "Besides, I've made enough terrible decisions today based on sleep deprivation and paranoia. Time to try making some good ones based on actually thinking things through."

AURORA

Hunter and Odion exchanged a look, then Hunter nodded slowly. "You're right. Much as I hate to admit it, we're not going to do anyone any good if we collapse before we find her."

"There's a small stream about a quarter mile east," Marina said, checking her tracking equipment. "Clean water, sheltered area. We could set up a basic camp, get some food in us, rest until morning."

"And plan our approach properly," Odion added, his analytical mind already working through the logistics. "Figure out exactly how we want to handle finding Aurora, what we're going to say to her, how we're going to get her out safely."

As they gathered their gear and prepared to move to the more sheltered campsite, Tobias found himself thinking about leadership again. Not the desperate, crisis-driven decisions he'd been making all day, but the kind of thoughtful, people-centered leadership that actually served his team.

CHAPTER TWENTY-THREE:
Aurora's Painful Choice

Aurora woke up to hands shaking her shoulders with urgent insistence. For a moment, she was disoriented; Raven had never woken her before, had always respected her need for uninterrupted sleep as part of the healing process. But the older woman's face was tense with concern, her weathered features tight with an alertness that immediately put Aurora on edge.

"What is it?" Aurora asked, sitting up in her simple cot and reaching instinctively for the earth magic that had become as natural as breathing.

"Intruders," Raven said quietly, her voice carrying the controlled calm of someone who had dealt with danger before. "My protective magic detected them entering the forest about an hour ago. Two people, moving with purpose."

Aurora's blood turned cold. After months of healing in this remote sanctuary, she'd almost forgotten that the outside world might eventually find them. She closed her eyes and extended her magical awareness outward, feeling for the disturbance Raven had sensed.

There. Two magical signatures moving through the forest below. Familiar ones.

"Sabrina and Lucien," Aurora breathed, her eyes snapping open.

AURORA

"But that's impossible. I thought they were dead. Captured by the authorities, at least."

"Apparently not," Raven replied grimly. "And if they're here..."

Aurora's heart clenched with sudden terror. "Tobias. If they found this place, if they're tracking magic users... oh god, what if they killed him? What if he's already—"

"Don't assume the worst," Raven said firmly, though her own expression was troubled. "Use your scrying. See what's happening."

Aurora nodded, moving quickly to the small basin of water they kept for just this purpose. She placed her hands on either side of the bowl and focused her magic into the clear surface, searching for any trace of the people she cared about most.

The images that formed in the water made her gasp with relief and fresh worry in equal measure. Tobias was alive, moving through the forest below with three companions—Hunter, Odion, and a young woman with blue hair that Aurora recognized with a pang of guilt. Marina. The girl she'd tortured for information, now apparently working alongside the people Aurora loved most.

"He's alive," Aurora said, her voice thick with emotion. "They all are. But they're following right behind Sabrina and Lucien. This could be a trap."

Raven moved to stand beside her, studying the images in the water with the practiced eye of someone who understood tactical situations. "Or it could be that both groups are tracking the same thing. You."

Aurora felt her magic stir in response to the familiar protective instincts, the urge to rush down the mountain and position herself between potential threats and the people she loved. But months of Raven's patient teaching held her back.

"I could take them," Aurora said, her voice carrying the old authority she'd once wielded without question. "Sabrina and Lucien. I've beaten them before."

"And start a magical battle in a foreign country where any of you could end up dead or captured?" Raven asked mildly. "That sounds like the old Aurora talking."

Aurora paused, recognizing the truth in Raven's words. The old Aurora would have charged down the mountain without thinking about consequences, would have solved problems through direct confrontation and overwhelming force. But she wasn't that person anymore. Was she?

"What do you suggest?" Aurora asked, settling into the patient mindset Raven had taught her for approaching complex problems.

"Watch," Raven said simply. "Learn what's really happening before you act. Understanding first, action second."

So Aurora watched.

What she saw through the scrying water gradually shifted her understanding of everything. Tobias wasn't frantically chasing threats or reacting to crisis. He was leading his team with careful consideration, asking for input before making decisions, showing genuine concern for their wellbeing that went beyond just mission success.

When they encountered a section of treacherous terrain, Tobias didn't just forge ahead or demand they push through regardless of risk. He called for a break, asked each team member to assess the situation, and worked with them to find the safest approach. Aurora watched in amazement as Hunter offered suggestions without trying to dominate the conversation, as Odion contributed ideas with quiet confidence instead of desperate-to-please anxiety, as Marina shared her expertise without defensiveness.

"This isn't the Tobias I left behind," Aurora murmured, unconsciously echoing Raven's teaching about observing without judgment.

"People grow when they're given space to do so," Raven replied, settling beside Aurora with her own cup of morning tea. "Sometimes the most loving thing we can do is step back and let them discover their own strength."

Through the scrying basin, Aurora could see that Lucien was using his magic to enhance natural obstacles. He was making streams run faster, destabilizing loose rocks, creating environmental challenges that looked natural but were actually magical sabotage. She frowned, noting how much his water magic had improved since their last encounter.

When the team reached a swift mountain stream swollen with snowmelt and Lucien's magical interference, Aurora expected to see the kind of rushed, poorly-thought-out crossing that had characterized their group dynamics before. Instead, she watched Tobias gather everyone together for a planning session.

"Marina, what do you think about the current patterns?" Tobias asked, his voice carrying respect for her expertise rather than mere politeness.

"The flow is stronger than it should be for this time of year," Marina replied, kneeling by the water's edge to test the current. "But there are still predictable eddies we can use. The water's been magically enhanced, but the underlying patterns are natural."

"Hunter, can you create stable stepping stones without risking everyone if the magic fails?" Tobias continued.

"Yeah, but they'll only be temporary," Hunter said, studying the stream with professional assessment. "Maybe ten minutes of stability before the water pressure undermines them."

"Odion, what's your read on timing and spacing?"

Aurora watched as Odion pulled out a small notebook (when had he started carrying a notebook?) and began calculating distances and flow rates with the methodical precision she'd always admired about him. But there was something different now, a confidence in his contributions that hadn't been there when she'd known him.

"If we cross in pairs, with Hunter placing stones just ahead of each team, we can minimize risk and time exposure," Odion concluded. "Marina should go first since she can read any changes in the current, then help guide the others from the far side."

"Agreed," Tobias said immediately. "Marina, are you comfortable with your injured arm?"

"I can manage," Marina replied, and Aurora caught the way she automatically flexed her left shoulder, recently healed but still tender. When had Marina been hurt? And why was she traveling with Tobias's team at all?

Aurora watched the stream crossing with growing amazement. No one person dominated the decision-making. Tobias asked for input and actually incorporated it instead of just going through the motions of consultation. Hunter offered magical support without trying to take over the entire operation. Odion contributed analytical thinking without second-guessing himself constantly. Marina shared expertise without defensiveness or the need to prove herself.

They worked together as equals.

"He's become the leader I tried to force him to be," Aurora said softly, "by learning not to force anything."

Raven nodded approvingly. "Leadership isn't about having all the answers. It's about creating space for everyone to contribute their best."

As the team took a rest break within a few hundred yards of Raven's shelter, Aurora found herself close enough to overhear their conversation through the scrying magic. What she heard broke her heart in the most beautiful way possible.

"When we find Aurora," Tobias was saying, his voice carrying hope and concern in equal measure, "I want everyone to remember that she's been through trauma. Whatever state she's in, whatever she needs, we support her choices."

"Even if she doesn't want to come back?" Odion asked gently.

Tobias was quiet for a long moment, and Aurora could see the pain the question caused him. "Even then," he said finally. "I love her enough to want what's best for her, not just what I want."

Aurora pressed her hands to her mouth, tears flowing freely down her cheeks. This was what she'd always hoped he could become: someone who loved without needing to control, who protected without suffocating, who cared without consuming.

"I just want her to be okay," Tobias continued, "whatever that looks like."

The words hit Aurora like a physical blow, not because they hurt but because they revealed the depth of change in the man she'd spent years trying to shape. He'd learned to love without possession, to care without control. Everything she'd tried to teach him through manipulation and force, he'd discovered on his own by being given the space to grow.

"The most loving thing I can do," Aurora whispered to Raven, "is let him keep growing."

Raven studied her with those knowing eyes that had guided Aurora through months of healing. "And what does that mean for you?"

Aurora looked around the shelter that had become her sanctuary, at the restored forest where her healing work had allowed new life to flourish, at the scrying basin where she could see the team she loved more than her own life preparing to continue their search for her.

"It means I leave," Aurora said, the words coming out steady despite the way they tore at her heart. "Before they get here. Before I can fall back into old patterns."

"Are you certain?" Raven asked gently. "This is not a decision you can easily undo."

Aurora thought about everything she'd learned during her time here. The memory work that had taught her to organize trauma without being controlled by it. The restoration magic that had shown her how to heal instead of harm. The painful realization that her love for Tobias had been built on need rather than respect.

"I can't love him back the way he deserves," Aurora said quietly. "Not right now. Maybe not ever. And he's learned to love without needing to be loved back in the same way. I won't take that growth away from him."

She stood and began gathering her few belongings; the simple clothes Raven had given her, the small journal where she'd recorded her healing work, a few seeds from plants she'd helped restore. Everything that mattered to her could fit in a single backpack.

"Where will you go?" Raven asked.

"I don't know yet," Aurora replied honestly. "Somewhere I can continue the healing work. Somewhere I can learn to be whole on my own instead of defining myself through protecting someone else."

Raven nodded slowly, then moved to a small wooden box Aurora had never seen before. From it, she withdrew a handful of seeds and a small vial of clear liquid.

"For your journey," Raven said, pressing the items into Aurora's hands. "The seeds will grow anywhere there's been magical damage. The tincture will help you stay connected to your own magical core when you're lonely."

Aurora looked down at the gifts, understanding the deeper meaning. Tools for restoration and self-sufficiency. Everything she needed to continue becoming who she was meant to be.

"Thank you," Aurora said, pulling Raven into a fierce hug. "For everything. For teaching me that love means letting go."

AURORA

"Remember," Raven said as they broke apart, "healing is not a destination. It's a practice. Keep practicing."

Aurora shouldered her pack and took one last look at the shelter where she'd learned to forgive herself, where she'd discovered that true strength meant knowing when not to use power. Through the scrying basin, she could see Tobias's team beginning to move again, getting closer to this place with every step.

Time to go.

Aurora used her earth magic to obscure her trail as she moved through the forest, ensuring that no tracking magic could follow her path. She'd learned precision over the months here, how to change things without leaving traces, how to help without being detected.

As she reached the edge of Raven's protected area, movement caught her attention. Sabrina and Lucien were approaching through the trees, following what looked like a magical tracking device similar to Marina's water-sensing equipment. They moved with the confident purpose of people who believed they knew exactly where they were going.

Aurora's first instinct was the old one: confront them, fight them, eliminate the threat through superior force. But months of Raven's teaching held her back. What would charging into battle accomplish? A magical fight in North Korea that could get everyone killed or captured? More violence and trauma for Tobias to carry?

Instead, Aurora crouched behind a cluster of trees and waited. When Sabrina and Lucien were close enough, she extended the smallest thread of earth magic toward their tracking device and gave it the gentlest possible adjustment. Not enough to break it, not enough to be detected, just enough to point them in the opposite direction.

Away from Raven's shelter. Away from Tobias's team. Away from Aurora herself.

Sabrina frowned at the device, then showed it to Lucien. "The signal shifted," she said with obvious frustration.

"Equipment malfunction?" Lucien suggested.

"Maybe. Or maybe our quarry is more clever than we thought." Sabrina studied the surrounding forest with suspicious eyes, but Aurora's concealment magic held firm. "This way, then. But stay alert."

Aurora watched them head deeper into the forest, toward the more dangerous border regions where their presence as unauthorized Americans would draw attention from North Korean patrols. They'd have to deal with natural consequences for their choices, but she wouldn't add magical violence to an already volatile situation.

The choice to avoid conflict, to solve problems through strategy rather than force, felt like the final proof of how much she'd changed. The old Aurora would have seen enemies and attacked. The new Aurora saw people making poor choices and simply...let them.

As Sabrina and Lucien disappeared into the trees, Aurora continued her own journey in the opposite direction. She moved carefully, using her restored earth magic to encourage new growth in areas where her previous breakdown had left scars, leaving the forest a little healthier than she'd found it.

"Some promises are kept by breaking them," Aurora said quietly to the mountain air, thinking of the vow she'd made to a six-year-old version of herself in her parents' living room.

She'd promised to keep Tobias safe. And now, finally, she understood that keeping him safe meant keeping him safe from her.

CHAPTER TWENTY-FOUR:
The Final Truth

The shelter materialized through the trees like something from a fairy tale. Stone walls built seamlessly into the mountainside, smoke rising from a small chimney, gardens that seemed to grow in perfect harmony with the surrounding forest. After hours of climbing through increasingly difficult terrain, following Marina's tracking equipment through wilderness that felt untouched by human presence, Tobias had begun to wonder if they would find anything at all.

Now, staring at this impossible sanctuary hidden in the mountains of North Korea, he felt his heart hammering against his ribs with desperate hope.

"This is it," Marina said quietly, checking her water-sensing equipment one final time. "The source of all the magical disturbances. Everything I've been tracking leads here."

Hunter moved closer to Tobias, his voice low and urgent. "I can feel her magical signature. Recent, but…" He paused, frowning. "But fading. Like she was here very recently but isn't anymore."

Tobias's stomach dropped. After everything they'd risked, after crossing international borders and nearly getting shot by guards, after weeks of searching and months of Aurora being missing, were they too late again?

Before he could voice his fears, the shelter's door opened.

The woman who emerged was unlike anyone Tobias had expected to find. She appeared to be in her fifties, with silver-streaked black hair braided down her back and weathered skin that spoke of years spent outdoors. She wore simple, practical clothing suitable for mountain living, and she moved with the calm confidence of someone completely at home in this remote place.

But it was her eyes that caught Tobias's attention: dark, knowing eyes that seemed to take in everything about their bedraggled group in a single glance. Eyes that held no surprise at finding four exhausted foreigners standing outside her door.

"You're here for Aurora," she said simply, her English accented but clear. It wasn't a question.

Tobias felt his legs nearly give out from relief. She knew Aurora. She'd been here. "Yes," he managed. "We've been searching for months. Is she all right? Is she here?"

The woman's expression softened with something that looked like compassion mixed with sadness. "I am Raven," she said, stepping aside and gesturing for them to enter. "And we have much to discuss."

The interior of the shelter was as surprising as its exterior, comfortable but simple, with handwoven rugs covering stone floors and shelves lined with books, herbs, and what looked like carefully tended magical implements. A fire burned warmly in a stone hearth, and the entire space radiated a sense of peace that seemed almost magical in itself.

"Please, sit," Raven said, indicating cushions arranged around a low table. "You look exhausted. When did you last eat?"

"We're fine," Tobias said quickly, though his stomach chose that moment to growl audibly. "We just need to know about Aurora. Is she here? Can we see her?"

Raven moved to a simple kitchen area and began preparing tea. "Aurora was here," she said carefully. "For several weeks. But she is not here now."

The words hit Tobias like a physical blow. "What do you mean? Where did she go? When?"

"She left this morning," Raven replied, her voice gentle but firm. "Before you arrived."

Hunter leaned forward, his expression intense. "Did she know we were coming? Did something scare her away?"

"In a manner of speaking, yes," Raven said, bringing a tray of tea and simple food to the table. "She knew you were close. She chose to leave."

Tobias felt the world tilt around him. "She ran away from us? Again?"

"She made a choice," Raven corrected quietly. "A very difficult choice, made out of love rather than fear."

"I don't understand," Odion said, speaking for the first time since they'd entered the shelter. "If she knew we were coming to help her, why would she leave?"

Raven settled into her own cushion, studying each of their faces with those penetrating eyes. Her eyes settled on Odion. "Because sometimes the most loving thing we can do for someone is protect them from ourselves."

Tobias shook his head, frustration and exhaustion making his voice sharper than intended. "That's not love, that's cowardice. Aurora's been running away from problems her entire life. I thought she'd finally learned—"

"She has learned," Raven interrupted firmly. "More than you know. Aurora spent months here healing from trauma that nearly destroyed her. She learned to organize her memories, to control her magic, to understand the difference between protection and possession."

"Then why isn't she here?" Tobias demanded. "If she's healed, if she's learned all these things, why did she run away the moment we showed up to help her?"

Raven stood and moved to a small wooden chest near the window. When she returned, she carried a sealed envelope that she placed carefully in front of Tobias.

"She left this for you," Raven said simply.

Tobias stared at the envelope like it might explode. His name was written on the front in Aurora's familiar handwriting—neat, precise letters that brought back memories of a thousand shared moments. Lesson plans she'd helped him write. Notes she'd left on his desk. The careful documentation that had kept their magical community running for years.

With shaking hands, he opened the envelope and unfolded the letter inside.

My dear Tobias,

By the time you read this, I will be gone. I know how that must hurt, and I'm sorry for the pain my absence will cause you. But I hope, in time, you will understand why this is necessary.

I have spent the last several months learning things about myself that I should have understood years ago. With Raven's help, I have come to see that what I called love was often control, and what I called protection was often possession. I have been carrying a promise I made as a six-year-old child—a promise to keep you safe—and I have used that promise to justify a lifetime of decisions that were more about my needs than yours.

Through scrying, I watched your approach to this place. I saw how you have grown as a leader, how you make decisions with your team instead of for them, how you have learned to love without needing to control. You have become everything I always hoped you could be, precisely because you were given the space to discover it yourself.

AURORA

I realized that the most loving thing I could do was ensure you continue to have that space.

You don't need me, Tobias. You never needed me the way I convinced myself you did. You have built something beautiful with the people around you. A real team, a real family, based on mutual respect rather than dependence. I will not poison that with my presence.

I know you will want to search for me. Please don't. This is not me running away from problems; this is me finally solving the biggest problem I've ever caused. I cannot love you the way you deserve to be loved, not yet, and maybe not ever. I cannot be around you without falling back into patterns of control that would hurt us both.

But please know that I do love you. I love you enough to want what's best for you, even when that means I cannot be part of it. I love you enough to finally keep the promise I made to your parents properly. By protecting you from the person who has hurt you most.

Thank you for coming to find me. Thank you for caring enough to cross oceans and borders to make sure I was safe. Thank you for being exactly the person I always saw in you, even when my methods of trying to help you find that person were so wrong.

Take care of yourself. Take care of the family you've built. Let them take care of you. Trust your instincts; they are so much better than you think they are.

Someday, when I have learned to love without needing anything in return, when I can be around you without the urge to guide or protect or control, I will find you again. Until then, know that you carry my love with you always, even if you cannot carry me.

All my love,

Aurora

Tobias read the letter twice, then a third time, tears streaming down his face with each pass. The words blurred as his vision clouded, but the meaning was crystal clear.

"Oh, Toby," Hunter said softly, and suddenly Tobias found himself pulled into a fierce embrace. Hunter's arms wrapped around him as Tobias finally let himself break down completely, sobbing into his friend's shoulder with a grief that felt like it might tear him apart.

"She's really gone," Tobias managed between sobs. "She's really not coming back."

"I know," Hunter murmured, his own voice thick with emotion. "I'm sorry. I'm so sorry."

They stayed like that for long minutes, Hunter holding Tobias while he grieved the loss of someone who was still alive but had chosen to disappear from his life. Marina and Odion sat in respectful silence, their own eyes bright with unshed tears at witnessing such raw pain.

When Tobias finally pulled away, he felt empty but somehow cleaner, like crying had washed away something he'd been carrying for too long.

"I don't understand," he said to Raven, wiping his eyes with the back of his hand. "How is abandoning the people who love you an act of love?"

Raven's expression was infinitely patient. "What would you have her do? Return to your community and gradually slip back into the same patterns that hurt everyone? Stay close enough to you that she feels compelled to guide your choices, manage your decisions, protect you from consequences?"

"She could learn to do better," Tobias insisted. "She could work on changing those patterns while staying connected to us."

"Could she?" Raven asked gently. "When someone's entire identity is built around being needed, how do they learn to love without possession while remaining in the presence of the person they're possessive about?"

Tobias opened his mouth to argue, then stopped. He thought about his own journey over the past months—how he'd grown as a leader, how he'd learned to trust his instincts, how he'd built genuine partnerships with his team. All of that growth had happened while Aurora was absent. Would it have been possible if she'd been there, offering guidance and protection at every turn?

"She's loving you the way you deserve to be loved," Raven continued. "Without conditions, without needs, without strings attached. She wants your happiness and growth more than she wants her own comfort. That is perhaps the purest love there is."

Marina spoke for the first time since entering the shelter, her voice quiet but steady. "I hated her for what she did to me. The torture, the pain, the violation of everything I thought I was. But watching her choose to leave rather than risk hurting people again..." She paused, seeming to search for words. "That takes more strength than staying would have."

Odion nodded slowly, his analytical mind working through the complexity of the situation. "She's breaking a cycle," he said thoughtfully. "Taking responsibility not just for what she's done, but for what she might do. It's... actually kind of brave."

Tobias looked around at his team, at the people who had risked everything to help him find Aurora, who had crossed international borders and dodged bullets and exhausted themselves because they cared about his happiness. Hunter, who had betrayed his former allies to stand by Tobias's side. Marina, who had saved Odion's life and taken a bullet meant for Tobias himself. Odion, who had nearly died from magical exhaustion trying to help with this search.

They were his family. Not because Aurora had brought them together or because they needed him to take care of them, but because they had chosen each other. Because they worked together as equals, supporting each other's strengths and covering each other's weaknesses.

"You're right," Tobias said finally, his voice hoarse from crying but steadier than it had been. "She is loving me the way I deserve to be loved. And I..." He paused, the realization hitting him with surprising force. "I think I finally understand what that means."

Raven smiled with what looked like pride. "Understanding is the first step toward accepting."

"It still hurts," Tobias said honestly.

"Of course it does," Raven replied. "Grief is the price we pay for love. But pain doesn't mean the choice was wrong."

As they sat in contemplative silence, sipping Raven's tea and processing the emotional weight of Aurora's decision, Odion found himself studying their host with growing intensity. There was something familiar about her mannerisms, the way she tilted her head when thinking, the precise way she chose her words. Her approach to explaining complex emotional concepts felt like an echo of something from his childhood, though he couldn't place exactly what.

"You seem to know a lot about trauma recovery," Odion said carefully. "About memory magic and healing techniques."

"I've had experience with both," Raven replied simply.

"What kind of experience?" Odion pressed, though he wasn't sure why the question felt so important.

Raven hesitated for the first time since they'd arrived, something flickering in her expression that looked almost like... recognition? But that was impossible. They'd never met before.

"Memory magic," she said slowly, "is sometimes the only way to survive unbearable pain. When someone you love is better off without you, when your presence causes more harm than your absence, sometimes you have to... file away the memories that would make staying away impossible."

Something cold settled in Odion's stomach. "File them away how?"

"Complete erasure," Raven said, her voice growing quieter. "Making yourself forget they ever existed, so you can function without the constant ache of missing them."

Odion's breath caught. The careful way she explained memory organization. The patient teaching style. The understanding of trauma responses. The way she moved her hands when she talked, a gesture he remembered from dreams that might not have been dreams at all.

Odion took a deep breath, then said: "Hi, mom."

The Arcane Rebellion Book Three

About the Author

Denis James has a true passion for storytelling and immersive fiction. A (recovering) chronic depression and severe anxiety patient, Denis James writes with the intention of helping others who may be where he once was. When not writing, Denis can be seen teaching in his community, fixating on a book, tv show, or video game, planning travel, or being home with his family. (Or a combination of all of the above.)

Connect with Denis James:

- Facebook: Denis James – Writer
- Instagram: denisjameswriter
- TikTok: denisjameswriter
- Patreon: Denis James – Writer

Also by Denis James

Tobias – The Arcane Rebellion Book One

Hunter – The Arcane Rebellion Book Two

The President's Choice – Safety & Security

The President's Choice – Honesty & Transparency

www.ingramcontent.com/pod-product-compliance
Lightning Source LLC
LaVergne TN
LVHW041931070526
838199LV00051BA/2776